WALL OF CROSSES

A NOVELLA

BAJ GOODSON

BAJ GOODSON LLC

PRAISE FOR BAJ GOODSON

"It caught me off-guard…It's such an interesting critique of the human psyche, and of the dark reality behind these vicious cycles within family dynamics. We want a happy ending, but we don't get it, because that's not what this story is about. It's tragic and raw and hurts to look at, yet we can't help but stare."

ADELAIDE THORNE | Author of the *Whitewashed* Series

"…this story will grab you from the very first word, raising questions and slowly revealing [family secrets] until the final page. Just when one might think there could not possibly be more skeletons in the closet…you will be thrown for a loop so huge your stomach will drop."

ASHLEY BAKER | *Ashes Books & Bobs* Blog

"What kind of secrets do families keep from one another? Are there truly some that should never be revealed? What is family actually worth? These are some of the very hard, and often times uncomfortable, questions that Goodson brings up in her debut novella."

C.E. CLAYTON | Author of *The Monster of Selkirk* Series

"Secrets upon wickedly delicious secrets!"

JESSICA SHOOK | Author of *Shrapnel*

"Warning: this book will shock your socks off!…The Tamblyns are just…Wow. You gotta read it. You just gotta. You'll never look at people the same."

BECKY MOYNIHAN | Author of *Reactive*

"The way the mysteries and the secrets were crafted pulled me in so completely. And the characters! Hooboy, I haven't read a book that has every. single. character fleshed out, from their strengths to their very real flaws and weaknesses…You won't want to miss this one."

ALLISA WHITE | Editor and Writer

"A page-turner that kept me reading late into the night…and stayed with me much longer. Goodson explores both the better and the darker side of human nature in this compelling novella."

DAPHNE TATUM | Reviewer and Writer

"The ending stuck with me…and because the characters felt so real, I had to remind myself 'They're not really out there living these lives and secrets,' and that makes it one of my favorite books so far this year."

ZAI BELL | Reviewer and Writer

"Goodson wrote a flawless (and I do mean FLAWLESS), edge-of-your-seat suspense novella that will leave your mouth hung wide open with surprise when you've turned the final page."

MEGAN LUKER | Reviewer

Cover image by Issam Hammoudi

Cover layout and design by Josh Guilbeau of Reform Design

http://reformdesign.weebly.com

Printed in United States of America

Published by Baj Goodson LLC

https://www.bajgoodson.com

baj@goodsoninnovations.com

❀ Created with Vellum

CONTENTS

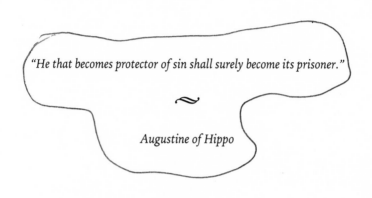

"He that becomes protector of sin shall surely become its prisoner."

~

Augustine of Hippo

CHAPTER ONE

"DEATH FIRST."

PONYTAIL SLASHING the air like a savage pendulum, Andy pivoted at the open doorway of the old house and tried to make a break for it—but Jacob Tamblyn was too quick.

"Not so fast." He watched his wife's expression go from apprehensive to mortified as he put a hand on her shoulder, holding her gently in place on the porch.

"This is where you tell me you're kidding and the real house is one of those pretty ones down the street, isn't it?" Her eyes pleaded with him to agree, to laugh and say, "aw, man, you got me", but when Jacob said nothing, he knew Andy's hopes were effectively murdered.

It had a been a rough few weeks for both of them, but today would mark the beginning of a whole new stress category. Jacob was at least thankful that they were taking it on as a team, that he could be the strong arms to hold Andy together, to squeeze her in that hug-you-until-you-suffocate kind of way that she always claimed made her anxiety more bearable.

He pulled Andy into him, burying his face in the top of

her head just as the dam of her emotions burst open in a flood of tears. The grapefruit scent of her shampoo enveloped his senses as her hairs tickled his nose; it was a welcome respite from the powerful stench wafting from the open front door: must and moth balls, laced with an undercurrent of some unprecedented mystery smell.

"It'll be okay," he said as Andy shook against him. Any time his girl cried, Jacob's heart took a beating; it was something akin to being hooked up to a taffy pull, twisting and stretching in wide, eternal circles. "Focus on the good part, babe—we have a brute squad. Extra muscle for days."

"Don't you kn-know what happened when the buz-zard gave the m-monkey a ride on his b-back? The buz-zard tried to eat h-him."

"What does that mean? Is that a story I should know?"

"Don't ask me stu-p-pid questions right n-now!" Andy screeched as more tears came, her wet face pressing deeper into Jacob's neck.

"Aw, Andy—"

"No! This is a c-c-catastrophe just waiting to hap-pen! *That's* what I m-mean!"

Jacob squeezed his wife's shoulders. "I admit that this will probably be ground zero for World War III. But look at it this way: we're the first ones here. That gives us time on our own to get a head start. Not so bad, right?"

"Stop try-ing-ing to put a posi-t-tive spin on this. We'll n-never f-finish this! Es-specially with your f-family here."

"Look at me. Please?"

Her overflowing eyes were swollen and red when she raised them to Jacob's, making his chest ache further as she rumbled against him, sobs hiccuping.

"Andy, I don't like this any more than you do. But we have no choice." He wiped away several fat tears, his thumbs gentle as they swept beneath the world's prettiest set of eyes.

"Tell you what. Let's do your breathing exercises for a sec; you'll feel better."

"Brea-thing exer-c-cises will only make me m-more aware of the smell in h-here."

He tried not to laugh at that. "C'mon, let's give it a try."

"No." She swatted at the fresh teardrops marring her rosy cheeks. "I'll be fine, I p-promise. Just...hold me a little l-longer."

Tightening his arms around her, Jacob savored the way they fit together like two puzzle pieces. He'd never get enough of this. "We'll get through this, you and me. Piece of cake."

As Andy decompressed, she gradually became less rigid in Jacob's arms. She always struggled to pull herself together after an anxiety attack; it was a painful thing for him to witness.

When her breathing began to slow, he pulled away to better see her face. "Think you'll be all right?"

"I guess I have to be."

Jacob delivered another squeeze to Andy's shoulders before releasing her. They stood side by side, observing their surroundings more closely. Still sniffling, Andy gripped Jacob's arm as though siphoning his strength into herself.

"There's just so...*much*," she said. "Why didn't we get the memo that he was a hoarder?"

The couple hadn't moved far beyond the front door, remaining in the large foyer that stretched into a hallway so long it faded into an abyss of pitch black. But as far as the eye could see into the dark, with the exception of two very tight walking paths to the living room and kitchen, every square inch of floor space was packed with *stuff*.

It looked like the worst estate sale known to man: discolored baskets and rusty pails, ragged umbrellas, folding lawn chairs with holey fabric, ancient coffee makers, space heaters, and fans, boxes galore—it barely skimmed the surface. Dust motes danced like fairy guardians above it all, backlit by rays of light let in by the open front door.

"Don't know how anyone could live in these conditions." A wretched feeling stirred in the pit of Jacob's stomach—it resembled guilt, and the moment he realized it, he shoved it down deeper where it was easier to ignore.

"What are these marks on the floor?" Andy disentangled herself from Jacob to poke her head into the equally cluttered living room, her eyes on the floor, following the thin streaks in the dust. They traveled on what was obviously a forced path from the front door, through the foyer into the living room, and to the base of the staircase leading to the second story.

Jacob, having looked over her shoulder, sighed. "Coroner. They rolled the gurney in and out."

"Oh." Andy shivered. "I shouldn't think about that too hard. This place already gives me the heebie-jeebies." She wrapped her arms around her waist. After a glance upward, she pointed to the ceiling. "There's a light fixture above us. Do we have electricity?"

"It was never shut off. There should be a switch over here somewhere...." Jacob maneuvered himself with painstaking slowness at the edges of the cramped space before them, trying not to knock anything over. It was several minutes before a light popped on overhead, bright enough to outfit an interrogation cell.

Seeing spots, Jacob plodded back to Andy. "We should get started. As they say, 'We're burning daylight'." He peeled off his jacket and hung it on a wall sconce, then set to rolling up the sleeves of his flannel overshirt.

Andy followed suit. Jacob watched as she took notice of the impossible number of decorative crosses lining the walls behind the mile-high stacks of boxes and junk.

"Whoa. These are beautiful." She ran her fingers across one that, by the look of it, was carved by an intricate hand out of driftwood. "Was he very spiritual?"

"Didn't used to be. Maybe he was towards…the end."

"Well. That's a heck of a lot of crosses for somebody who wasn't."

"Maybe he had a ghost."

Andy shoved her husband's arm. "Are you *trying* to give me another anxiety episode?" The tape on the uppermost box to her right was coming loose, and she yanked it off, tugging back the flaps. "Charming—a bunch of wiring for electronics. They aren't even organized, just thrown in helter-skelter."

"Toss 'em. Let's say all trash boxes go on the porch, and the men and I will move them to the street at the end of the day." Jacob began picking his way down the hallway past the foyer. Even with his cautionary steps, his foot caught the edge of a tower of old cassette tapes that came crashing to the floor. With a sigh, he bent down and raked them together to assemble a new tower. Before placing the last one on top, he opened the cracked plastic case on a whim.

"I think these are all empty…."

"Empty? Are you sure?"

In answer, Jacob opened multiple cases—each one turning out to be just as unoccupied as the first.

Andy cocked an eyebrow. "That's kinda weird."

"Yeah." Jacob raised himself to his feet. "Doesn't matter, though." His throat constricted, gut rattling with the unruly pest of contrition. He turned from his wife, reminding himself of the goals at hand. "I'll try the kitchen for some trash bags—it's just through here. Holler if you need me."

The kitchen was no better than the foyer, living room, and hallway—more piles of newspapers, overstuffed boxes, random junk, and what appeared to be moldy garbage strewn across the floor. The sight was enough to make Jacob want to hurl, a sensation that wasn't helped by the formidable increase of that smell, like something rotten. Jacob fitted the neckline of his undershirt over his nose and mouth in hopes it would block some of it out, but the effect was insignificant enough that he opted to tough it out.

This light switch was easier to get to, and the second Jacob flipped it on he heard the skittering of minuscule feet, making him jump as his eyes searched warily for the source.

"Something wrong?" Andy called.

"Rodents." Jacob didn't miss Andy's unsettled whimper before he continued, "Haven't seen them yet, but there're droppings everywhere. They've been here awhile."

"Fantastic" was all Andy said.

"Keep an eye out."

Jacob went first to the table, a large rectangular farmhouse style that had been built long before trend outweighed practicality. Its wooden surface was buried beneath mounds of any and all kinds of clutter. A thick layer of dust coated everything, suggesting the mess had been undisturbed for some time.

How did he last as long as he did?

The question entered Jacob's mind repeatedly as he panned over pile after pile of rubbish. Some made sense, such as mail, magazines, and more recent editions of the local newspaper; others, however, left Jacob shaking his head as he balked over preserved candy bar wrappers, expired packets of ketchup, discarded batteries with the casings removed, tea lights with black stumps for wicks, wire, string, guitar picks, and dried up pen refills.

"Anything interesting besides rat turds?" inquired Andy from the foyer.

"Nope. More tributes for the garbageman."

"Same here." Andy sucked in an audible breath, making

Jacob pause. "I just found a box full of naked dolls. What kind of a creepfest is this?"

Jacob felt a pang of discomfort, more of that bothersome guilt leaking into his limbs. A sharp inclination to defend John's memory reared its head, but he let it die in silence. "Put it on the porch."

He hadn't spent much time in this house when his grandparents were alive; they were nice people, sure, but his relationship with them was a sad, anemic thing. They weren't exactly the t-ball game cheering section type (or even the graduation ceremony cheering section type). They sent him cards for big occasions, though. They were always signed by "Granddaddy and Gamma", but that sounded so...*casual* to Jacob. When he was around them, it had never felt casual at all. In fact, in his own mind, he hadn't referred to them as anything but their names: John and Betty.

Dropping the last heap of mail he'd browsed, there was no doubt in Jacob's mind that further perusal of the kitchen table would be a waste of time.

They're not in here.

He made a move for the built-in drawers in the cabinetry, but froze mid-stride when he heard the same skittering as before. Out the corner of his eye, something rustled a dishrag near the sink. He snapped his head that direction, but whatever had been there was already gone, disappearing with ease behind the masses of debris layered atop the counters. There was a dismembered wooden handle of an old toilet plunger within reach; with a burst of forced bravery, he used it to pry open one door at a time to all the cabinets, providing a wider berth between him and any creatures who might jump out upon having their nest exposed.

The stale air in the room stirred with every opened cabinet, piercing Jacob's mind as if with willful, steel-tipped fingers, dragging their way through his nostrils and up his sinus cavity, stabbing through the remaining barriers to his brain. *You allowed this to happen*, they accused. But Jacob, his determination growing and expanding like a seed plant, banished the cries again and again, refusing to let them stifle his own will.

Several times he heard the tiny feet in motion again, but he never did see the critters themselves. He did, however, find a box of trashcan liners, and a sealed plastic bag with a tattered pair of lawn gloves, one crusty dishwashing glove, and two packs of sanitized surgical gloves. He shouted his findings to his wife.

"Thank God! My hands are already turning gray."

Taking a long, regretful look around the shabby kitchen, overwrought with a strange sense of melancholy and nostalgia from his younger days, Jacob took the lawn gloves for himself and brought Andy one pack of the surgical gloves.

He steered his expression away from his thoughts as he said pointedly, "We'll leave the cruddy dishwashing one for somebody else." He winked.

Andy's returning grin was wide. "I can't wait to see your mother dig around in this crap with *that*. It's almost enough to give up our part of the inheritance."

Jacob dipped his chin at her. "Almost."

☦ · ☦ · ☦

For a time they toiled in the foyer like worker bees, buzzing this way and that, focused and driven. The conversation was minimal and confined to the task, until Jacob returned from relocating a box to the porch to find Andy thumbing through what appeared to be a leather notebook.

"Hey, what's that?"

"Not sure, but I think it may have belonged to your

grandmother." She glanced up, her smile eager. "Kinda cool. It's a journal or something."

Jacob squished a spider under his shoe as he scooted some boxes around. "Journal, huh? Does it have a year?"

There was a lengthy pause before Andy replied, "Um, yeah. It looks like she, uh, chronicled her decline."

Going very still, Jacob repeated, "Her...decline?" The fine hairs on the nape of his neck stood on end as Andy held out the journal.

"Take it."

His mind tumbling, mouth full of cotton, Jacob clasped his fingers around the leather spine, bringing it to his side without looking at it. He licked his lips. "I should—I'll look at it later."

"Okay." Andy dropped her face to the floor, giving him a moment.

Jacob didn't like feeling as though someone had just spooned out his insides like a jack-o-lantern. He ran a solitary finger across the cover of the journal, still holding it at his side, eyes fixed on nothing. "They both lived in this house for so long. I knew I'd come across stuff like this." He gulped. "I thought—*hoped*—I was ready."

"Oh, babe." The instant Andy's hand made contact with his shoulder, he sprang out from under her touch.

"Sorry—I'll just put this in the car." Jacob hurried from the house toward the parked car in the driveway, his heart thumping like the bass drum of a morbid marching band.

CHAPTER TWO

AFTER AN HOUR OF working in near silence, there was a thud outside. Jacob peeked out the beveled glass of the front door to see a distorted car in the driveway behind theirs, its equally distorted owner trudging up the sidewalk toward the house.

He faced Andy, his hand already on the knob. "Someone's here. You ready?"

She whipped off her gloves and ran her hands over her hair before straightening her clothes. "How's my makeup? No raccoon eyes, right?"

With a crooked grin, Jacob responded, "You look perfect."

Andy smirked. "Shut up and open the door, you moony-eyed love letter."

Jacob filled his lungs with musty air and pulled back on the heavy wooden door, cool autumn air wafting in and blowing his hair straight up like a blast from a leaf blower.

Uncle Larry stopped short when he saw Jacob. Then he laughed, slapped his round belly, and continued up the porch steps. "For a second there, I thought I was looking back in time at your daddy."

"I get that a lot." Jacob knew his smile didn't meet his eyes. It wasn't that he disliked his uncle, but what lay ahead of them would be undertaking enough without adding small talk to the equation.

"Nice to see ya, kid." Uncle Larry gave Jacob's shoulder a firm clap. "And who's this?"

Andy stepped forward. "We've met before, but I changed my hair. I'm Jacob's wife."

His small eyes lit with recognition. "Ohhh, yeah, yeah, I remember now." Then his smile faltered as he offered his hand. "Is it...Andrea?"

"Everyone calls me Andy."

"Then Andy it is—and I like the hair." He winked, but then stood awkwardly in the doorway, looking to Jacob with reluctance. "So. Can I assess the damage?"

"Please." The couple stood back and Uncle Larry strode past them into the foyer, immediately struck by the smell as they had been.

"Gosh a'mighty," he sputtered as one bear paw of a hand went over his nose. "That's a real treat, ain't it?"

Jacob shrugged as he closed the door. "You get used to it. The kitchen's worse."

"There are rodents," Andy added with feeling, her mouth twitching in aversion.

Uncle Larry stiffened, glancing around uneasily. "I see. Lord, I hate them things." He absorbed all the boxes stacked around them, sniffing and grunting with further distaste, then picked up a dusty, yellowed newspaper with tentative fingers. "'November 5, 1982'," he read. "Shoot. The whole house like this?"

"We haven't explored beyond here and the kitchen yet," said Jacob. "As you can see, it's been more than enough to keep us busy."

"Mind if I take a look around?"

11

"Be our guest," said Andy, her face betraying her unwillingness to join in any such adventure. "It's your house now anyway."

Uncle Larry exchanged a meaningful look with Jacob, but Andy had already resumed opening boxes. "Nothing but coupons." She sifted through what must have been a thousand clipped paper coupons for grocery and household items. "Why would they hold on to these things? Most of these have been expired for years."

"It's common for folks who lived through the Depression," said Uncle Larry, "even those who were youngsters at the time."

"Some of the stuff gets pretty weird." Jacob showed Uncle Larry the boxes on the porch that Andy had already gone through, and Uncle Larry grunted again.

"Hmm. Bizarre." He scratched his balding head and ambled back inside with Jacob at his heels. "And the crosses," he noted, pointing to the decor on the foyer walls, "I don't remember seeing those before. I wonder what brought that on."

"Jacob suggested a ghost had taken up residence here, and these were to help ward it off or something," Andy commented derisively as she opened another box. "Ugh, worn out shoes. Did John and Betty know nothing about junk stores that take this kind of crap?"

Uncle Larry laughed, a bitter sound. "They surely did! Most of mine and Dirk and even Ruthie's clothes growing up came second-hand. More of that Depression mindset at work. Pinching pennies. You think those coupons were bad...."

"Speaking of depression," Jacob quipped, "any idea when the others are coming?"

Uncle Larry's bulky shoulders lifted and fell. "Dirk couldn't get off 'til eleven, and you know Ruthie...will or no will, she'll take her time getting here. Not that she'll be much help anyway once she does grace us with her presence." He cast a tired look heavenward. "We'll go it alone a good while, I'd wager."

"Probably for the best." Jacob spared a grimace for Andy, who wrinkled her nose.

"I wouldn't be hurt if she stayed home," she mumbled.

Uncle Larry cackled. "Oh, she'll be here, mark my words. She wants that inheritance, and if this is how she gets it, a Cat 5 twister couldn't keep her away."

Jacob handed one pair of the good gloves to his uncle before heading back down the hall. "I'm off to the back rooms if you care to join up, Uncle Larry."

"Hey! You really leaving me out here by myself?" complained Andy.

"Relax. We'll be able to hear you scream if the ghost comes for you."

"Wow, thanks a lot. My hero." Andy worked her way through the tape of another box, muttering to herself as the men retreated down the hall.

Uncle Larry found the light switch for the hallway, flooding their surroundings with light. More living things skittered as the shadows shifted.

"Great," they said in unison, leading each of them to chuckle companionably.

Plucking their path through the debris was slow-going. Uncle Larry stumbled over some balls of yarn that were spilling out of a collapsed box.

"So, Jake," he said in a hushed tone as he attempted to unravel the loose ends of a yarn ball that had tangled around his foot, "I don't mean to pry into your personal business here, but is there a reason you haven't shared the news with your wife yet?"

Jacob didn't answer immediately. He focused his eyes on a

dull painting of a flower garden that was mostly obstructed by boxes.

"It's complicated." He sighed. How could he explain to Uncle Larry things he couldn't find the words to explain to Andy, the person who meant more to him than life itself? "Everything's happened so fast...I haven't had the right opportunity. This is a lot to take in, and she's already stressed. She had an anxiety attack just walking in the door here."

"Can't say I blame her. I kinda feel like having one myself. She gets those attacks a lot?"

"They come and go. Lately they've been worse because of...well, a little bit of everything, I guess."

Admittedly, Andy wasn't half as stressed as she would've been had she known about their debt, made worse by Jacob's pay cut, courtesy of the demotion they'd hit him with at work two weeks ago. Even before that, for several years he and Andy had been struggling financially, but Andy had no clue. It was Jacob who kept up the books, and he hadn't had the heart to tell her about the numerous credit cards he'd maxed out on bills, the close calls on the car payments, the last chance notices on the door of their apartment. Andy was his free-spirited dreamer, and he would do everything he could to shield her from those mundane worries.

Really, he would have told her about the demotion when it happened—but she'd been in the middle of interviewing for a new job. If it played out, Andy would have a $14,000 raise, and a significant decrease in fuel costs with her commute. She had been so elated at the possibility. What kind of husband chose a time like that to come clean to his wife about money problems? Turning up the pressure would have only frayed her nerves.

No. He'd decided to put off telling her just until she was out of the extended interview process, no big deal.

That was days before the news of John's death came, and with it, news of the will. Jacob's hope was renewed. It was only a matter of time before their financial situation would be righted again—all he had to do in the meantime was keep them afloat until the lawyer released the funds.

Uncle Larry kicked away the yarn at his feet and continued down the hall with Jacob. "I get it," he murmured, "and you know *I* won't say anything. But I hope you've thought about what could happen when your momma gets here...." Using his hands and fingers, he pantomimed a make-believe explosion, complete with boyish sound effects.

Crestfallen, Jacob groaned inwardly. Ruth was always the kicker, wasn't she? He'd thought about Atomic Ruth in passing, always assured himself there was still time to tell Andy, or at least to find a solution to bypass Ruth blowing the whistle on him—but he had come up with nothing, and Andy still didn't know the truth.

"Something to think about," he remarked aloud.

"So shouldn't you tell Andy before then?"

"I'm thinking about it." Something in Jacob's voice must have indicated to Uncle Larry that the conversation was over, and he swallowed the words he'd been poised to speak.

The men came to the end of the long hall where they were met with three closed doors—one on either side of them, and one straight ahead. Jacob picked his way to the latter and turned the knob, surprised when it was unlocked. He'd always assumed this door led to the cellar, but as a child, he'd been too scared to find out. He had snuck into one too many horror movies in his efforts to avoid going home in a hurry when he could manage it. Even slasher films seemed mild compared to his mother on bad days.

Obviously avoidance was his personal method of choice for dealing with conflict.

"That's just a linen closet," Uncle Larry informed him.

"Probably more junk in there." And there was. Spiderwebs covered every visible corner, and there was nothing special from what Jacob could see.

"What about these rooms?" he asked.

"Not sure what they did with them recently, but when I last was here, these rooms were Ma's. She used one as a sewing room, and the other as a lady lounge for when she wanted alone time. It was her happy place, you could say."

"Which is which?"

Uncle Larry pointed to the left door. "That one's the sewing room. Bet there's some equipment in here that could fetch a decent re-sell price." Uncle Larry tried the doorknob and it, too, was unlocked. The door cracked open but was hindered by something on the other side, so he could only push it partway back. "Lemme get a look-see at what we've got in here."

"I'll try this other one."

Jacob found nothing keeping this door from opening. The room was shrouded in murky darkness made possible by the layers of heavy curtains over every window. As he stepped inside, the ungodly smell caught him full in the face, much like it had in the kitchen, but this was far more potent. He felt bile rising up his windpipe before he could cover his mouth and nose.

He felt along the wall past the doorframe for the light switch, but when he flipped it, nothing happened.

"No lights in here," he voiced to the others, though both were so caught up in their own pilgrimages that they didn't seem to hear.

Even in the dim glow allotted from the cracks at the bases of the curtains, Jacob could see this room was different. He could only make out the shapes of furniture, but on the far outer wall there were mostly windows, providing greater visibility of the silhouettes against them. There was a small bookshelf behind a tea table that sat between two chairs, along with several vases with dead flowers. The floor around it all was bare but for rugs.

Compared to the rest of the house, this room seemed almost unaffected by change. For some reason, John had left this room as it was when he'd stockpiled the rest of the house with strange treasures.

Jacob could imagine Betty in here, the curtains pulled back to let in the sunshine, a thoughtfully-selected book on her lap as she sat in one of the chairs and poured herself a cup of tea from the tea service.

He had barely known Betty—his Gamma—but he'd always remember her how she was during his parents' divorce when he was eight. She'd sat with him outside the courtroom one day, her blue-veined hands a bit frightening as she offered him a peppermint, but something about her warmth and kindness made him feel less overwhelmed, as if life wasn't quite so excruciating after all, and there were still reasons aplenty to eat peppermints without worry.

As Jacob moved deeper into the room with the intention of drawing back the curtains, his attention was brought to a long table in the center of the room. It took up a startling amount of space. To Jacob it seemed out of place, yet there was a sense of being very purposeful in its position.

An animal instinct within Jacob rose onto its hackles as he inched toward it, noticing the foul smell strengthening with every step. A violent sinking in the depths of his navel, Jacob identified a sheet shielding an odd shape along the expanse of the table. Every hair on his body extended, and a cold shiver raced up and down his spine.

He called in a miraculously steady voice toward the hall, "Everything good, Uncle Larry?"

"Yeah," came the gruff reply, "just trying to move things around so we can get through the door better."

"Need help?"

"Nah, I got it. Thanks, kid." There was a pause as Uncle Larry seemed to take a break; Jacob could hear his heavy breathing. "What about you?"

Jacob sucked in a silent breath of his own and called, "Still looking." With a hand that faintly shook, Jacob pulled back the edge of the sheet.

"Holy—!"

A surge of vomit shot up his throat, nearly choking him as he flung the fabric down and wheeled around for the door. He slammed it shut behind him.

Uncle Larry clambered towards the doorway of his own room and leaned against the door, as he still couldn't fully open it. "What is it?"

Andy shouted from the other end of the hall, "You okay? What happened?"

"No one go in there. I mean it. No one at all." Jacob knew he was breathless, but it was all he could do to keep the vomit at bay.

Uncle Larry's forehead crinkled with his increasing frown as Andy yelled back, "Why? What's in there?"

"Just don't go in. Believe me."

Seconds passed before Andy trilled, "Oh *gawd*, you found the rodents!" When Jacob didn't respond she exclaimed, "Ugh, you really *did*, didn't you?! Ew, ewewewew!"

"I'll take care of it," said Jacob.

"I don't care what inhumane thing you have to do, just get rid of them!"

Uncle Larry started to offer his assistance—though, based on the cringe he could scarcely conceal, it was more out of manly duty than a desire to be helpful—but Jacob cut him off.

"Thanks, Uncle Larry, but I've got this." In a lower

volume he added, "I should handle the bigger messes. They're my problem now."

With only the briefest interlude, Uncle Larry nodded once and went back to his task in the sewing room. While he worked, Jacob went in search of the ring of keys he'd seen somewhere in the kitchen earlier. It didn't take him long to find it again, and he immediately traipsed back to the closed lounge door.

It took some time to find the right key to fit the lock, but eventually he walked away from a successfully locked door. He was sure to place the keys in the pocket of his jeans for safekeeping before he rejoined Uncle Larry. His heart still hammered in his chest, but his breathing was almost back to normal.

"Gave you a good start, did they?" snickered Uncle Larry when Jacob entered the sunny room; there were no curtains on these windows, the first room in the whole house so far that wasn't shut up like a tomb. The thought gave Jacob chills, which only made Uncle Larry laugh outright.

CHAPTER THREE

RUTH ARRIVED AT ELEVEN. Andy and the men had just widened the walking path in the living room and exposed the tall windows when the doorbell sounded.

Andy stuck her head into the foyer, shouting, "Come on in!"

The doorbell rang again as though in a last-ditch effort to give fair warning. *Run far away, while you still can!*

Opposed by every cell in her body, Andy mustered up a neutral expression as she yanked the front door open for her mother-in-law.

On the porch, Ruth stood erect as a monument, her chin cast down as she flicked a leaf particle from her spandex workout clothes. Only when she'd finished did her eyes find Andy; as if by mechanical automation, each woman pressed her mouth into a tight smile that matched the other's.

"Well, I'll be," Ruth said. "Andrea, in the flesh. That's one heck of a surprise." Her country twang was far more pronounced than Jacob's, but it was in the same camp as Uncle Larry's. "Figured the likes of you would be too tied up for such a mundane family chore as gutting a dead relative's house."

How paradoxical, coming from you, Andy wanted to retort, but she bit back the words, allowing them to melt into her esophagus with a sharp pinch. Ruth probably wouldn't know what 'paradoxical' meant anyway. "I'm here to do my part, like everybody."

Ruth raised cosmetically tattooed brows. "Cute. Where was that attitude when we were all at the funeral you missed?"

Andy could feel her face heating, but she swallowed the stone in her throat with authority and looked away. "As Jacob told you before, there was a mandatory work thing I couldn't get out of. It was bad timing."

"Bad timing, uh huh." Derision set Ruth's jaw, but faded into a sickly-sweet smile. "Heaven forbid someone die when it's inconvenient for you." She waved a hand and shifted her weight on spindly legs. "I just can't help thinking that if it'd been *your* grandfather, you would've moved mountains to be there. But hey, maybe that's just what I would do."

"Ruth," Andy began, her fingernails slicing into her palms as she made fists behind her leg, "if I could have been there, I would—"

"No, no, I get it, Andrea. Work trumps family—even when you get the house, apparently. Congratulations on that, by the way. Clearly you deserve it."

Get...the house? Blinking, Andy stumbled backward, the movement opening the door wide enough so that Ruth could slip by her into the foyer where she was met by Jacob and Uncle Larry.

"Well, well, if it ain't my wicked son and my turd of a brother. How ya doin', boys?" She swept Jacob into her arms for a hug that looked very uncomfortable, then released him and acted as if she planned to do the same to Uncle

Larry—but at the last second, she popped his forehead with the palm of her hand in an odd, childish manner that sent his head reeling back. Then she waltzed past him to examine the mess of the house.

"This place is looking sorry." A look of repugnance swept over her features as she covered her nose, the smell registering with her more slowly than it had the others; Andy assumed her sense of smell was all but gone after years of smoking like an industrial chimney. "Gads, what a stink."

"You get used to it," said Jacob, his voice detached.

"Well. If it were up to me, you can bet I'd knock this dungheap to the ground and sell the plot. But I know my way of doing things is unpopular with this crowd." Ruth gave a pointed look to the others before she scrunched her nose a few times and reached into the leather purse at her hip. She pulled out a tube of lipstick, wasting no time in locating a mirror on one of the decorative crosses and using it to apply a fresh coat to her lips. The color was too bright for her, Andy noticed, shrinking her already thin lips.

When she finished, she gazed at the entirety of the wall with its many crosses, making a "hmph" sound. "My folks were always weird birds."

"Ruthie, take it easy. They were old and alone." Uncle Larry swiped at his forehead as though it itched, skin still pink where his sister had whacked him. "Cut 'em a little slack. They didn't dog on you for being a black sheep, you know."

Ruth set falsely wounded eyes on her brother. "Black sheep? C'mon, Larry. I was the only one out of all four of their offspring to amount to much."

In the background, quietly going through her breathing exercises, Andy straightened. As far as she'd known, Jacob's mother had only two brothers. Was there really another?

But what a trivial thing in light of what she'd just learned about the house; she reminded herself of that, launching back into her exercises.

Uncle Larry folded his arms over his barrel chest. "Be fair, Ruthie—only three of the four count for the last thirty years."

Thirty years? What in the world were they talking about?

"Even before Patsy died, I was hitched with a bun in the oven, Larry—and I didn't even do it out of order."

Patsy? There used to be a sister? Andy's eyes swung to Jacob, pulse swelling in her ears with every heartbeat. *What else have you kept from me?*

Uncle Larry huffed. "Dirk ain't here yet, so you can save the javelin jabs from your high horse."

"I got nothing to prove to Dirk anyhow," said Ruth. "It's *you* who's got the big problem, always judging me and my affairs."

Uncle Larry leaned toward her with a sarcastic smile. "Fine choice of words."

"There you go again! Means nothing to you that I finished high school and took college courses, got a job, even made a little cash. There's lots to be proud of, the way I see it."

"Colorful perspective. I'm sure your kid here's got no complaints whatsoever about your life of virtue. Huh, Jake?" Uncle Larry nodded in Jacob's direction but didn't wait for an answer. "I'll bet he *loved* being raised by a momma with *three* husbands. And ain't like you was any good at actually *being* his momma—was she, kid? Gotta be free to fly, always. Ain't that right, Ruthie?"

Andy fought not to roll her eyes as Ruth cooly brushed some rogue dust bunnies off her immaculate Nike running shoes. "I do like my freedom—I'm big enough to admit it." She turned to Jacob now, studying his face. "But I didn't *neglect* you. I'm a much better parent than my brother, Dirk, for instance. I never left you. Did I, Jake? Aren't I better than that lowlife scum?"

"Ruthie!" Uncle Larry blustered, his jowls shivering.

"I'm staying out of this. Come on, Andy." Jacob dove through the gap between his mother and uncle and laced his fingers through Andy's, guiding her into the living room. "Good time to check out the upstairs."

"Yeah," Ruth cooed after them, "why don't you two get a feel for your new home? Maybe break in the beds?"

Jacob's jaw tensed, and Andy had a sudden vision of him spinning around and boxing his mother in the mouth.

But Uncle Larry's immediate response to Ruth's barb was like a protective barrier between them and her, turning Ruth's attention to her brother when he hissed, "Will you never grow up?"

"Me?! You're the one living in the same trailer he bought at age twenty!"

"At least I own something. I started saving my earnings when I was *ten* to buy my place, and there ain't nobody to take it away from me! Can *you* say that, Little Miss Divorce Court?"

"I have property!" spat Ruth. "And are you bragging on the fact that you're sixty-one-years-old and still *single?*"

"You're single, too, black widow!"

Ooh, nice one! As she and Jacob climbed the immense staircase, Andy couldn't help being a tiny bit invested in the argument, living vicariously through Larry as he met Ruth blow for blow.

"Ain't a one of my exes dead, Larry," said Ruth. "And look at this body—at least I got options. What do you got? A shiny bald spot, squinty eyes, and a gut that'd make a potbelly pig green with envy, that's what!"

Uncle Larry spluttered, and Andy felt a twinge of sympathy on his behalf. "Some women don't care about that stuff!"

"Puh-*lease!* Is that how you get yourself out of bed in the morning, with that pep talk? 'Larry is a winner!'"

Their raised voices could not be escaped even on the second story of the house, but as soon as they were out of earshot, Jacob piped up with an apology.

"I'm so sorry. They've always bickered like children, but *that* was embarrassing."

With fresh distance between them and the scene downstairs, Andy's frazzled mind grappled with everything that had happened in the last few minutes. Then her thoughts processed their way through the mire to the most pressing of issues. Not bothering to bridge the gap between topics, she fixed her gaze on her husband's and said slowly, "When your mother got here, she said it was you and me getting the house—and *don't* tell me she's a nutcase and brush it off. She sounded like she knew what she was talking about."

Jacob held his breath. He had tried to prepare himself for this moment, but even with all the staged conversations he'd had with Andy in his mind over the past two weeks, nothing seemed to fall in line with what he wanted to say. Now he'd have to wing it.

He scratched the stubble on his chin and tossed his head. "Look. I didn't know how to tell you this, but I didn't really sign the papers on that apartment last week." He felt his wife stiffen beside him, her fingers between his hardening like slender stones. "But before you freak out on me, you should know that it's because we don't *need* that apartment anymore."

The edge of Andy's mouth quirked as it did whenever she was fighting to subdue strong emotions. Many of her attacks began with this look, and Jacob placed a hand on her cheek, willing her to be more surprised and excited than surprised and angry.

"What does that mean?" she croaked, the rhythm of her breath picking up speed.

"It means...you're standing in our new home."

"Excuse me?"

Jacob took both her hands in his. "This house is ours, Andy. I sort of inherited it from my grandfather."

Andy pulled away, putting physical distance between them. Her chest was heaving now.

Jacob rushed to go on. "I didn't expect it, Andy. It's not like I was close to him—how could I have known?" He found her hands again, forcing them back into his own; her jaw clenched, and she looked away from him. "But I should have told you. When I got the call from the lawyer, I shouldn't have waited. I take full responsibility for that."

"Then why did you wait?"

Jacob had hoped to somehow magically avoid that question. His tongue went tacky, sticking to the roof of his mouth as he responded, "There was so much happening in our lives already, and you were...so anxious. I didn't want to make things worse."

His answer was not acceptable to Andy; her face turning the color of a plum made that clear. "This is crazy. And to have to hear about it from your *mother* of all people, Jacob! *Ugh!*"

"I know. I know, and I'm sorry."

"How long have you known?"

With a hard swallow, Jacob said, "Two weeks."

"Two weeks?! Jacob, I'm your wife—your *wife!* That warrants transparency between us, doesn't it? Or is it naive of me to think I can trust my own husband?"

"Andy, I'm sorry, okay? I really thought it was better this way." Jacob wanted to pull his hair out, punch the wall, *some-*

thing that would vent some of this frustration. "I was planning on telling you today, before my mom could, but I'd already waited so long—I couldn't find the right words. Everything sounded stupid in my head." He ran a hand over his face and sighed. "I just want you to have everything you deserve. Does that make me such a bad guy?"

A long stretch of silence passed. Andy began a breathing exercise, and when Jacob tried to join in for good measure, she shoved him away, continuing on her own with a dark look. She paced in front of him for what seemed like a lifetime, until at last her demeanor softened in the slightest, and she took a small step toward him.

"I'm sorry."

Jacob started. *"You're* sorry?"

"Halfway sorry. You weren't too far off base—partially, anyway. It was stupid of you not to tell me, and I'm super pissed about that. But this *is* big news, and with my new job, I know I've been disconnected." She shook her head. "But at the same time, Jacob, I have to ask—what were you thinking? Taking on this house? It belongs in a landfill! And someone *died* here! No amount of sentimentality should drive a guy as surefooted as you into a black hole of debt, and definitely not for *this*. I don't know what you're trying to do here." Her eyes were twice their normal size as she put a hand to her forehead, beginning to pace again. "Say I could get past the corpse thing. This is still a huge house, and it needs an insane amount of work. It'll take a lot of money to make it livable, and even then, where would we stay in the meantime? Is there a mortgage? And what about our current lease? There's no way our savings can handle this!"

Black hole of debt. Corpse. Savings. Jacob steeled his expression against the turmoil raging inside of him, pushing past the words that cut him into ribbons, focusing instead on soothing his wife's panic. He placed his hands on either side of her waist, stilling her, thumbs coursing over her shirt in delicate patterns. This woman, she was the life he had chosen, the essence of all he held dear; he would cling to that until there was nothing left.

"Andy, listen to me. Those worries make sense, but I've already thought of them all. For starters, I've been paying special attention to the house as we've been clearing out the junk, and if you can believe it, it's in awesome condition—pristine, even. It's just dirty, needs a little TLC. Yes, it's also out of date, but get this: John left an extra remodeling fund for whoever accepted the house, and my great-grandparents willed this house to my grandparents when they died, so the mortgage is long paid for. It's not the bank's—it's ours!"

"Are—Are you kidding?"

"I have the paperwork to prove it."

Andy's eyes seemed to glaze over as they swept across the drab paneled walls, the dusty floor, the raggedy wallpaper and discolored rugs, the cobwebs that seemed to multiply every time you looked away. She leaned against the closest wall with a *thunk*. "Wow. Just...*wow*."

Jacob watched her face, missing nothing as emotions chased each other across her features. Not a word was spoken between them for a long time, until Andy coughed, her hand going over her throat as if it was closing up on her.

"You okay?" Jacob asked in alarm, afraid she was having another attack.

"I...I think so. I just can't believe it. And you know something? I'd be even closer to my new office than the new apartment would have been."

"That's true."

"And we'd be homeowners. No more rent that goes toward a long-term *nothing*." A tremor of excitement shook her voice.

Jacob's mouth twitched in anticipation of a smile. "You're right."

"So, what? We clean it up, give it an update, and move in?"

"Sure. Shouldn't take *that* long to get it livable, then we can move in and do the rest slowly. Make it less overwhelming, huh?"

Andy sucked her bottom lip in between her teeth. "What about your family? Aren't they interested in the house?"

Jacob almost laughed at that. "Not even a little bit."

Andy's brow crinkled in that way that had first enticed Jacob to her, before they'd even met. For a succulent moment, he was transported back to that sidewalk cafe in downtown Austin, mesmerized by the cute girl across the street outside the candle shop, watching as she picked up jar after jar of candles lined up on a table outside, sticking her nose into them one by one and making such an inconceivable range of expressions that Jacob couldn't wait to see what her face would do next.

"Hold on," she said suddenly. "Uncle Larry. I'd just assumed—He's the oldest, why didn't the house go to him in John's will?"

Jacob tucked his shoulders back and shrugged. "According to the lawyer, it *did*. Then it passed to Dirk, then to me. But Larry and Dirk don't want it. They don't have wives, or kids—well, that speak to them, in Dirk's case—and they're already comfortable where they are. They're simple men with simple lives; this was too big a project for them. They were fine with just their inheritances."

"I don't understand. Why not sell it and divide the money among the relatives? Isn't that what most people do in this kind of situation?"

"If that were allowed, I'm sure they would have. But the will was explicit—whoever accepted the house couldn't sell it. And if anyone tried to legally contest, they would get nothing at all. Apparently my grandparents really wanted this thing to be passed down to another generation or two."

Understanding dawned on Andy's face. "That's why your mother was such a pill to me. More so than usual."

"She thinks it should have passed to her before it passed to me or even to Dirk, since she's older than him, but apparently *Granddaddy* had a different idea. She's jealous, like always."

"But your mother hates this house! She said so herself— said she'd knock it to the ground and sell the plot. We all heard her!"

Jacob nodded. "You're not wrong."

"So she just doesn't want anyone else to have it?"

"What do you think?"

"This is too much, Jacob." Andy pulled him down the wall with her, the two of them landing on the hardwood floor at the same time as they pressed their backs against the wallpaper of faded wildflowers. The smell up here wasn't so bad, but they could still hear Ruth and Uncle Larry swatting insults back and forth like a game of badminton.

"Why *did* we get the house over her?"

"I don't know. I can't pretend to make sense of it, but the will was clear." Jacob's words sounded as if they were being squeezed through a rubber tube as he played with his thumbs in his lap, an acidic bubble growing in his throat.

Andy rested her head on her husband's shoulder, wrapping one arm around his. "I guess if she cared anything about being reasonable, then she wouldn't be Ruth." Jacob kissed her temple, and the warmth of his breath on her face reminded her of all the reasons why she loved this man.

She'd known from the moment he walked into her life that Jacob Tamblyn wasn't like the other guys she'd met at the university. She would never forget how certain she was of it, and she'd been certain of it every day since.

The day he had swept her off her feet like the noblest of Prince Charmings, she was changed. She had been in a sour mood, taking a personal day off work and school to walk the streets in downtown Austin for a pick-me-up after another rejection letter for yet another internship. She'd stumbled across a quaint little candle boutique, their clearance display outside all but calling her by name as she tried to walk past. She must have spent half an hour smelling every single one, but three times she went back to Ginger Apple, its spicy scent almost as good as teleporting home to Florida, straight into her mother's kitchen at the height of pre-holiday pie-baking. It had gripped her senses so tightly that she could see Corey, her brother, elbow deep in flour as he worked on their mom's legendary pie crust, his help invaluable with those massive piano-player hands.

She'd come close to buying the candle; she'd even gone inside the boutique with it once, but then she'd turned around and put it back, urging herself to walk away. Several blocks later, she was regretting her decision and contemplating the walk back to the boutique when she heard a man's voice calling, "Hey, excuse me. Excuse me. Hey!"

Curious, she glanced around, and that was when she saw him: a man with bewitching gray eyes so open and friendly it hit her in the chest like an arrow as he jogged breathlessly after her, a gift bag in hand.

"Are you talking to me?" she squeaked at him as he drew up to her, throwing one finger in her face as he bent over and gripped his knees, winded.

"Um…are you okay?" she asked in concern.

"Oh—I'll be fine. You're just—wheeeew, you're a fast

walker. Very fast. Wow!" He heaved himself up, planting his hands on either side of his waist, the pink gift bag sticking out at a sharp angle. "And I'm painfully—*so* painfully out of shape."

"I'm sorry?" Andy didn't know what else to say to that. She stole a glimpse around them; no one was in their immediate area, but she could see a police car parked some distance away, and she made a mental note. "Can I help you with something?" Gripping her purse a little tighter, she eyed the man with great suspicion.

He didn't look dangerous, but most serial killers didn't, right? He was dressed like many of the college students she saw on campus, in a *Keep Austin Weird* t-shirt and shorts. She caught sight of a distinct scar topside of his right wrist, shaped like a goldfish cracker. Good. Something like that could help her identify him in a lineup if things went south.

Still panting, the man smiled sheepishly and thrust the pink gift bag toward her. "Here."

Andy stared at it, blinking.

"It's for you," he said.

"Me?" Astounded, Andy took a step back. "But you don't know me."

His gray eyes found hers then, and she was suddenly without breath. "Please. Take it. It's from that candle shop a few blocks down."

"Candle...?" It dawned on her then that he must have been watching her before, outside the candle boutique, and she chanced a panicked look at the police car.

"Don't worry, I'm not a creep or anything. I, uh, was just eating lunch at the cafe across the street, and you were making funny faces while you smelled the candles, and— heh." He cleared his throat and gave an awkward shrug. "Anyway. You didn't buy it, but I could tell you wanted to."

All at once, Andy understood, and her jaw flopped open.

Not without trepidation, she reached for the bag he still held out to her. She pulled back the tissue paper just enough to peek inside—sure enough, there was the Ginger Apple candle, in the largest size available. Slowly lifting her gaze back to those round gray eyes, she felt a smile overtaking her lips.

"You…bought this for me? A stranger?"

The man shoved his hands into his pockets and suddenly found the concrete very fascinating. "A pretty stranger with an interesting face. Sure."

"You think my face is interesting?"

"And pretty." He was trying not to smile, and so was she. The more they both tried, the more they failed, until each of them shook with giggles.

"I'm Jacob, by the way. I like sandwiches." As soon as the statement left his mouth, he raised his face to the clouds with an expression of utter regret. "And clearly I've lost my mind if any part of me thinks that sounds like a cool thing to say about myself."

Andy erupted into more giggles, propelling her open-faced hand into the space between them. She was embarrassed by how she was acting, not normally so silly with boys; but there was something different about this one, and he'd caught her off guard. "Andy. I like candles."

"Hi, Andy who likes candles." Jacob's hand swallowed hers, but it was warm, and softer than she'd expected. "So. Why didn't you buy the candle?"

"Oh. Um, it made me think of home." It was her turn to find distraction in the concrete at their feet. "I've been feeling kinda homesick lately, and…I was trying to be strong."

Jacob surprised her by staying silent. Those gray eyes held her fast as though everything in the world had dissolved, and all that remained was her. It gave her a feeling that baited her breath in her lungs as if by a spell.

When she managed to tear herself away, she dedicated her focus to the pink bag Jacob had given her, its bright hue blinding in the midday sun. "That probably sounds stupid," she realized aloud.

"Not at all." He'd wasted no time in saying it, and when she peeped up at him through her lashes, she could tell he meant it. "But for the record, I bet you'll be strong anyway—even with the candle."

Andy chewed her lip, her stomach alive with bustling butterflies. It had been a long time since a guy had made her feel this giddy, and she couldn't deny that it was intoxicating.

Jacob tipped his head to the side, one corner of his mouth turning upward. Those fathomless eyes seemed to sparkle. "Listen. I just ate at the cafe, but if you're up for coffee...."

And that had been it for her. Coffee had turned into drinks, drinks turned into dinner, and dinner had turned into history.

Jacob had romanced her from the very beginning, his gestures both grand and small forever surprising and touching her in every way possible, winning her over with the sweet sincerity of what was purely *him* again and again.

"You know, I hope you like it in this house, once it's fixed up. I want you to have everything in the world, Andy."

The hallway of the old house swirled around her as Andy laughed, amused that her reverie was interrupted by a statement so fitting. She leaned into her husband, their noses resting against each other. "Such a hopeless romantic. Is there no mountain you wouldn't climb to make me happy?"

"I will always do whatever it takes."

As Jacob tucked a strand of hair behind Andy's ears, she surged forward with a kiss. When they broke apart, it may as well have been their first for all the flutters it awakened in Andy. "I love your impossibly big heart, Jacob Tamblyn."

Downstairs, Ruth was all-out screaming at Uncle Larry

now. The scratchy peal of her smoker's husk grated against Andy's eardrums with every taunt like a wire brush snagging satin fabric, dampening the mood.

"If she gets out of line, says *anything* that upsets you, I'll make her leave," Jacob said suddenly.

Andy felt his goldfish scar under her fingers, as familiar to her now as her own reflection. "Thanks, babe, but if I can't get through one day with your mother, I won't be able to live with myself."

Jacob released a puff of air that resembled a laugh and stood up, holding his hand down to her. "Let me know when you change your mind."

CHAPTER FOUR

"ANYBODY ORDER A PIZZA?"

Jacob observed with a touch of amusement how out of place his Uncle Dirk's toothy grin was when he entered the gloomy house around noon. Dirk's chipper cadence seemed to make the shadows shrink in on themselves—but only until Ruth appeared from the living room.

"One pie for five people? I hope you already ate." Blowing her frosted bangs away from her eyes, she clomped over to him and snatched up the flat box from his arms.

"Ruth, you do have to share that," said Jacob. He hated having to say such things to a grown woman, but alas....

"Back off, Jake" was his mother's response.

Dirk's jaw went slack as he gawked at Ruth and then at Jacob, who shrugged and rolled his eyes. "Nice day to you, too, Ruthie."

"Don't pretend you care how my day is," she barked back.

"There's actual calories in that pizza, you know." Uncle Dirk's eyes had a mischievous twinkle. "Wouldn't you rather have a salad? I saw dandelions out front with some other green weeds—I could whip you up a rabbit food feast."

"Don't start with me, Dirk! Jake won't let me smoke in the house."

Jacob scoffed and said scathingly, "You've been smoking all day."

"It's carbs or nicotine, and I prefer both when I've gone too long without either."

"She's been smoking all day," Jacob insisted to Uncle Dirk. His attempts to keep his emotions off his face were failing at the moment, he knew; Ruth had an annoying habit of bringing out the worst in him. But Uncle Dirk winked conspiratorially, and the small act reminded Jacob he wasn't alone.

Uncle Larry came towards them from the long hallway as he removed his gloves. There were dark splotches of sweat soaking through his shirt in multiple places. "That's the most reasonable thing you've said all day, Ruthie. You gonna do like your boy said and share with the rest of us? The grub, that is, not the nicotine."

"Doughboy! You'll put a sock in it, too, if you know what's good for you!" Ruth glared at all three men as she lifted her chin and pranced toward the front door with the pizza box under one arm, and an unlit cigarette hanging from her saturated upper lip.

"Where you going with that?" asked Uncle Larry in a tone that said he was prepared to roll up his sleeves and wrestle her for his share.

"I ain't eating in here with that god-awful smell, are you crazy?"

"Well, fine, but don't you be hogging that pizza, you hear? The rest of us gotta eat, too."

Ruth snorted with laughter. "Right. Says the size 42 to the size 4. You could use to skip a few meals, Larry."

The moment she disappeared onto the porch, everyone's shoulders relaxed.

"Thanks for the food, Dirk. Good timing, too. We could use a breather, that's for darn sure." Red face punctuating the words, Larry mopped his glistening forehead with a sleeve and patted his younger brother on the back.

"Sure thing." The rugged features of Dirk's face contorted as he added, "but gol-ly, she's right about that smell. It's worse than a skunk's funeral parlor in here. Straight churns my stomach."

"You get used to it." It didn't escape Jacob's notice that he'd said this to every newcomer.

"I can see why Ruthie don't wanna eat in here. Shoot, it's making my eyes burn!"

"Oh, can it, bonehead." Ruth came back through the front door, grabbing a metal folding chair that was propped against the wall underneath the display of crosses. Her cigarette smoldered, a fine wisp of smoke trailing above her head as she moved. "Who can eat in peace with you griping and complaining like a six-year-old?"

"Try not to listen, then." As she vanished once again with her chair, Dirk ducked his head, almond eyes rounding. "Ears like a dang bloodhound. I forgot about that."

Skirting around the exchange, Jacob said, "The smell isn't as strong upstairs; that's where you'll be after lunch, Uncle Dirk."

"Thank God for that." He scratched the back of his head, gazing around his former home with an increasingly sullen expression. "Wow. I sure didn't expect this. The place looks mighty rough."

"It looks better than it did, believe you me," sighed Uncle Larry. "We've been hard at work lugging stuff out."

"I saw the porch. I just don't understand it...Pop was never like this before."

Jacob's heart tugged at that. Guilt wrapped its claws

around him once more, and he pressed his lips together so firmly his teeth broke skin.

"When's the last time you was here?" Uncle Larry asked Dirk.

"Ain't sure. Before Ma's funeral, maybe? So less than two years ago. Didn't look nothing like this."

"Did you see them crosses over there? How about that, huh?"

Uncle Dirk's wave-tousled head swung around to face where his brother pointed, and his brows rose. "Interesting," he said slowly, taking them in with a look of dismay. "Guess losing Ma really turned Pop's priorities around."

Larry sniffed, his red face turning purple. His voice wobbled as he said, "We should've been here with him, Dirk. We could've stopped this. Just look at this mess!" He spread his arms, gesturing around them, and swayed from side to side as he fought off his afflictions. "I can barely stand it, knowing he was living alone in squalor."

Jacob couldn't look at Uncle Larry anymore. He cast his eyes on Dirk in time to see him make a fist and put it to his forehead, closing his eyes.

"I know, Larry," he said miserably. "But we was doing what we always do, what he taught us by example—looking after our own problems."

An invader in a conversation that was better left private, Jacob murmured, "I'll leave you gentlemen to yourselves." He turned to go, seeking relief from his uncles' pain with a desperation that would have made weaker men tremble.

"Nah, Jake, don't—it's okay, son." Uncle Larry took a deep rumbly breath and brought his hands to his meaty hips. "It's just hard to see, that's all. Pop was so strong, and...the man who died here wasn't."

"Our Ma used to call him 'Ranger', did you know that, Jake?" Uncle Dirk queried his nephew.

Jacob shook his head.

"It was short for 'Lone Ranger'. He was independent as all get out. Taught her to be, too, and they raised up kids of the same inclination."

"All but one," chuckled Uncle Larry, seeming to come down off his outburst in stride. "Ruthie got hit with all our co-dependency and then some."

"Shh, not so loud," whispered Uncle Dirk with a half-cocked grin, eyes on the front door that was still cracked slightly ajar. "The Vampire Queen'll hear you and sic her bats on us."

The men cackled together covertly like middle grade boys on the cusp of trouble.

"I'm right glad y'all took the house, Jake," said Uncle Larry, smacking one of his giant bear paws against Jacob's back, nearly knocking the breath out of him. "Even though it's a pigsty right now, this old place could use a fresh start. I think you and your wife are just the folks it needs."

The bubble of guilt inflated painfully in Jacob's stomach, but he nodded his head and muttered, "Thanks, Uncle Larry."

"I think I'll head on upstairs, fellas—I'm ready to hit the ground running." His regular pep returning, Dirk started towards the living room, but Jacob stopped him with a hand that slapped hard against his uncle's solid torso.

"Ack!" Jacob shook his hand out with a grimace. "I was going to ask if you were hungry, but now that I know you eat bricks...."

"Shucks, I did throw back a load before I came—" Dirk cast a sideways glance in the direction of the unlatched front door, and finished in a whisper, "—which I'm now very thankful for."

"I think I'll join you upstairs." Andy approached from the kitchen, her ponytail flecked with dust and debris particles.

Jacob wasn't sure what she'd been doing, but he was glad she'd missed his uncles' moments of frailty.

She sidled up next to him long enough to whisper into his ear, "Save me a slice of that pizza if you can. I'll get it later when *she's* otherwise occupied."

"Uh oh, a kindred spirit." Uncle Dirk's expression glowed with his knowing smile, indicating he'd heard every word.

A blush heated Andy's cheeks, probably at having her private callousness toward Ruth exposed to a practical stranger, Jacob mused, but the warmth in Dirk's brown eyes seemed to melt her embarrassment away.

"It's Andrea, right?"

"Andy," she corrected as she shook Dirk's extended hand; she had to assume it was the handshake of a man whose common practice was to only shake hands with other men, because he gripped her so tightly she almost cried out. When he let go, she had to actively refrain from wringing the hand out right in front of him, good manners be cursed.

"Winner winner, chicken dinner," crowed the oblivious Dirk. "You can come along behind me and fix whatever I mess up."

Despite the handshake, Andy's answering smile was authentic. "Sounds like a plan."

As the pair passed through the living room to the stairs, Ruth could be seen through an open window nibbling at a sliver of pizza, her cigarette in the other hand, now a stub; its pungency wafted into the house on a breeze, mixing with the preexisting odor into an acrid cocktail.

At the top of the staircase, the smells mercifully began to fade as Andy showed Uncle Dirk into the bedroom that needed the most attention.

"You brought gloves. Good."

"Not my first rodeo." Uncle Dirk beamed, and something about his eyes when he did it struck Andy as familiar.

They set straight to work, making simple conversation as they went. Ruth made Dirk seem like a slimeball the way she talked about him, but Andy found him to be a teddy bear, warm and comfortable. She had only met Dirk once before, and she liked him as much now as she did then; he was certainly the most upbeat of his siblings. But when they'd exhausted all basic topics that required little personal knowledge of each other, Andy felt things leaning in the direction of awkward silence.

She wriggled out of one glove and removed her phone from her pants pocket. "Mind if I put on some tunes?"

"Oh—I'm *always* down for tunes." Uncle Dirk gave her another one of those grins as he kicked a couple of lightweight boxes across the floor toward the doorway.

Andy scrolled through her phone, in search of a good playlist. "You know, you remind me of someone. I keep seeing it, but I can't put my finger on who it is."

"Probably Jake. But don't let Ruthie hear you say so. She's always hated it when people say we favor."

"Yeah, I, uh, I've noticed she doesn't...play nice with family."

"Putting it mildly," laughed Dirk. "Ruthie has her own way of thinking, of doing things. But she knows what's proper and what ain't. She pretends otherwise until she can make somebody else look bad—like me, for instance." He removed each of his work gloves, flexing his black-stained hands as though they were stiff or sore. Andy noticed the severe calluses, too—whatever work he did in his profession, it may have made him lean and fit, but it wasn't easy on his body.

Before she could consider the appropriateness of such a question, Andy blurted, "Ruth has dirt on you?"

Thankfully, Uncle Dirk didn't seem perturbed by it in the least. "Yes and no. I'm an easy target because I got a past. It's public knowledge, and it was a long time ago, but the consequences were lasting. I won't quit hearing about it 'til one of us dies." Tossing his gloves aside, he tugged a big box out from under the bed, sending dust swirling up their noses. They both coughed and waved the air, prompting Andy over to the window, where she slid the drapes aside and forced the pane open for some fresh air.

Uncle Dirk lifted the loose lid of the box with one hand. "Well, I'll be."

Returning, Andy peered over his shoulder to see that this box was full to the brim with photographs. They weren't disorganized as most of the boxes had been, but neither were they protected by sleeves or envelopes.

Uncle Dirk removed a handful off the top and began flipping through them. "They'll be old. Been forever since we acted like a real family."

Andy saw a flicker of sadness in Dirk's eyes, but then it was gone. "Do you want me to sort them?"

"You don't gotta do that. The box has Patsy's handwriting on it; I'm willing to bet she had plans for these." He glanced around the room. "This was her bedroom, you know. Spent lots of time up here, even after she moved out."

Andy spared a moment to absorb what was underneath the initial clutter of the room. There was muted mauve wallpaper dotted with flower blossoms. The bed frame was made of rounded iron. The dresser was dingy but matched the rocking chair beside the bed. The wall mirror near the window had a slight distortion, and the crocheted rug beneath their feet was shaped like a rose. Signs of a real person having once lived here, having given it her personal touches.

"Uncle Dirk," Andy ventured, watching his face for any changes as she dared to ride the wave of good luck she'd had with her last bold question, "you don't have to answer this, but I've never heard of Patsy before today. Can you tell me about her?"

His answering sigh had a mournful quality to it. "Makes sense. The rest of the family don't bring her up much anymore. Jacob never met her—she died the year he was born, while Ruthie was pregnant. Anyway, Patsy was the oldest of us—already a teen when I came along." He paused, something in the box catching his eye. "Lookie here. A snap of when she was a kid...."

He showed Andy a black and white photo of a young girl with curly pigtails. She was eating a sandwich that dripped dressing down the front of her shirt as she sat atop a tractor as if she did it all the time.

"She was shy. Didn't make friends easy because she kept to herself a lot, but she was the kindest soul you'd ever meet. Loyal, dependable, patient. Ma doted on her, which made Ruthie boiling mad, of course."

"Sounds like Ruth." Recalling the comments Ruth had made earlier about Patsy, Andy imagined the posture of jealousy had always been present with Jacob's mother. "I assume they didn't have a great relationship?"

"Nope. Ruthie never had a nice thing to say about Patsy, stirred the pot at every chance, and Patsy just took it like a martyr. She was gracious, and brave—like our Ma. And Ruthie was...well, she was just Ruthie."

Andy pondered that about her mother-in-law, what a challenge it was to put her into words. The nature of strife, of finding contempt with anyone and everyone for the pettiest of reasons wasn't easily explained; and Andy was a victim of it herself. It was an entire year after she got together with Jacob before he allowed her a first meeting with the mother her then-boyfriend called "Atomic Ruth". When the day finally came, and Ruth laid eyes on Andy, she said on an airy sniff, "Jake, Jake, *Jake!* How many times do I gotta say this before you hear me? Find yourself a redhead; brunettes are a dime a dozen!" After the shock and hurt wore off, Andy learned that such statements were to be expected from Ruth, and set side by side with other things Ruth said to and about others, merely being slighted for her hair color wasn't so terrible.

"I feel sorry for all of you, having a sister like Ruth. Makes me all the more grateful for my brother."

"Ah, you got a brother? That's nice."

"Yeah. He's pretty great. I miss him."

"He ain't around here?"

"Nope," Andy replied wistfully. "He lives in Florida; that's where I'm from. But...I guess you could say he's my oldest friend." Strangely, Andy had never stopped to think about it before, but Corey *was* her oldest friend. She had a lifetime of memories with him dating back as far as she could remember, and even the worst ones were golden compared to what it must have been like to be siblings with Ruth.

"Wish Ruthie thought that about me," Dirk said. Then he laughed ironically. "Heck, I wish I thought that about her!"

Andy traced a finger across the monochrome image of Patsy, feeling a peculiar sweep of melancholy wash over her at having never met this woman of mild-manner and mystery. The thought even crossed her mind of how different Jacob's life may be if Patsy had been his mother instead of Atomic Ruth. "Hey, Dirk...If Patsy was the oldest, she would've been, what, in her thirties when she passed away? Wasn't she married by then? A mother?"

Uncle Dirk's mouth drew taut. "Patsy was a loner,

and she was a mite plain. It ain't your normal recipe for drawing in a fella." He wagged his head. "She didn't like the idea of being a bitter old maid, though. She graduated from college with honors, then worked like a dog at a desk all her days. But unlike the rest of us, she still came around plenty." He picked at a hole in his jeans, and sniffed. "Now I wish I'd taken a leaf from her book."

For a time, they both stared at the floor. Andy could hear Dirk taking breaths as though to speak, but then he'd stop, deflate, and stay quiet.

"What happened to her?"

His head rose slowly at Andy's question. He cast a long look out the window, focused on the patch of cloud-dusted sky visible over the neighboring rooftops. "It was out of the blue. She'd worked late, got home and microwaved a TV dinner for one. They found her two days later on the couch in her bathrobe with her fork still in her hand."

"How horrible." Andy's stomach pitched, her mind conjuring a facsimile, but of herself coming home to find Jacob that way. When Dirk didn't elaborate, she cleared her throat. "Again, you don't have to answer this if it's too painful, but how did it happen?"

"Brain aneurism. They've been known to touch our family tree. Doubtful she'll be the last."

"*Oh.*" Andy's breath left her in a rush, her lungs overtaken by the urge to collapse. "It's so tragic how much death your family has experienced."

"Life is a fragile thing." Uncle Dirk took one last look at the photo of Patsy, then dropped it onto the mattress. "That was thirty years back now. Hard to believe so much time's gone by. The world keeps on spinning, don't it?"

"I suppose it does." For some reason, that realization was more piercing than anything Andy had heard all day.

"Hey up there!" called a smoky female voice through the open window. "Is somebody in Patsy's room?"

Uncle Dirk rolled his eyes and yelled back, "What do you want, Ruthie?"

"Don't be throwing stuff away in there, you rattlesnake—I'm coming up!"

"Now why in tarnation would you wanna—"

"She's already gone. She can't hear you," Andy said with a sigh of resignation.

"That woman could make a nun swear."

Ruth came gliding in within minutes, her eyes hard enough to cut diamonds. "There're things that belong to me in this room," she announced icily.

Head tilted in a doubtful expression, Dirk prompted, "Like what?"

Andy noted that when Ruth set her gaze about the room, some of the color flushed out of her face. "There—that necklace!"

"The blue one on the dresser?"

"Yes! Patsy stole that necklace from me. It's mine, and I want it back."

Dirk pursed his lips. "She's only been dead for thirty years, Ruthie. You couldn't have taken it back before now?"

"Don't you dare make fun of me, you useless windbag," she snarled.

"Fine, then. I'm sure Andy don't want it anyway, do you, Andy?"

Andy shrugged. "It's not my style," she felt inclined to say, knowing this would prick Ruth's ego.

Sure enough, Ruth's eyes narrowed. She glanced at the necklace, and her lip curled. But she was not one to call 'uncle', especially not with an audience of two. She shoved her nose into the air. "There're empty Petri dishes with more culture than you, Andrea." She stomped to the dresser where she wasted no time in snatching up the necklace; but it had been laying there so long it had congealed to the dresser in some places, clearly not a piece of jewelry on the finer side, and the intensity of Ruth's movement snapped the necklace apart. Beads exploded across the room, each one of the surprised bystanders catching some in the face.

The series of yelps that ensued brought Jacob running into the room, a baseball bat poised in his hands. "What's wrong? More critters?"

"Hold your horses, Bambino," cried Uncle Dirk, "it was just a rogue necklace."

"Oh." The baseball bat came down. "What happened?"

"Your mother is a lunatic, that's what," Dirk said with a scornful look at his sister.

"Oh, bite me, you overgrown buffoon!"

"You sound better with your mouth closed, anyone ever told you that, Ruthie?"

Ruth bared her teeth as she hissed, "You think you're so gal'darn clever—!"

"Stop it, both of you," insisted Jacob, his free hand and the baseball bat each coming between his mother and uncle. "Ruthie, what are you even doing up here? The living room looks like a yard sale from the 80s puked in a recycling center and somebody tracked it home. Go back downstairs, would you?"

She crossed her arms over her narrow chest. "Not without my things!"

"What things?"

"The things Patsy stole from me!"

"Ruthie, just go back downstairs, *please*," pleaded Dirk, running a hand over his face so that the skin around his eyes was pulled down so far they could have rolled right out.

"I do need you down there, Ruthie," Jacob said diplomatically.

"You people are ridiculous." She tossed her hands into the air. "I—I can't stand to even be in the same room with you." A puzzling mixture of emotions warring on her face, Ruth took one last look around, then charged past Jacob and left the room as suddenly as she had entered it.

After the sound of her retreating footsteps had carried down the stairs, Andy whispered, "That was so weird, Jacob."

"Even for Ruthie, that was mighty odd," agreed Uncle Dirk.

Jacob let out a heavy sigh. "Sorry, guys. I'll let you get back to work now." He started for the door, then turned back, leaving the bat propped against the rocking chair. "Just in case," he said with a cheeky smile.

When he had gone, Uncle Dirk said to Andy, "Now where were we?" Returning to the box of photos on the bed, he brought out more snapshots, handing several to her after he looked at them.

She was thankful to pick up where they'd left off, but it took a moment for her mind to switch gears after the interruption from Ruth. Dirk was speaking for several seconds before she realized she'd missed what he said.

"Sorry, what?"

"I said these are of me. About middle school age, I reckon." He let out a dry chuckle. "I'm sorry, kiddo. Here I am talking your ear off like an old geezer when you probably don't care a lick about any of this stuff."

"Oh, no! Please don't think that, Uncle Dirk." Andy had been working to piece together what she could about her husband's family since she'd met him years ago. Her conversations with Dirk were the most fruitful she'd ever had, about anyone in Jacob's family. Every story Dirk told was news to her, and if going through old photographs with him all day meant she'd hear more about Jacob's family history, she'd do it. "I could listen to you forever."

"Really?" Uncle Dirk seemed unconvinced. "This isn't boring you?"

"Of course not," she persisted. "C'mon, tell me more. What else?"

Her husband's uncle scratched his stubbly chin thoughtfully. "Well, heh, okay, then." He flicked through the photos again, pulling out more of him as a pre-teen and early teenager. "They won't get much older than this."

"Why is that?"

"Because I left here as soon as I turned eighteen—just like Larry and Ruthie."

"And then...you didn't visit," Andy guessed.

Uncle Dirk's mouth sagged, and the light in his eyes seemed to dim. "Only rarely."

Andy felt his words like a blow to her heart. She could hardly fathom how he must feel, finding himself in the home he'd grown up in, decades later, closed in by regret from abandoning the people who raised him. The more she learned of this family, the more she could see the cracks in it that everyone else was so careful not to see. It wasn't that they were unaware the cracks were there, but no one wanted to think about them any more than necessary. It was their leading coping mechanism.

She asked, "May I?" and gestured to the box.

"Go for it."

She reached in and took out a stack for herself. The whole family at the fair, all the children climbing on a wooden fence, someone as a baby swaddled in a yellow blanket in their bassinet, one of the girls as a toddler scream-crying in a frilly red dress, one of the boys being held up by a disembodied pair of adult arms to put the star on top of the Christmas tree. It was all so normal.

When Andy found a snap of what had to be young Dirk squeezed between his parents on a porch swing, the three of them holding frothy glasses of root beer, she smiled and showed it to him. "This is a sweet one," she said. "We ought to find you a frame for this so you can take it home with you."

"Oh. Oh my—" There was suddenly a strangled sound in Uncle Dirk's throat that caught both of them off guard. "I— Oh, gosh." Turning his back to Andy, the filth forgotten, he seated himself next to the box of photos on the bed, a gray figure in a gray cloud against a gray room, as the metal mattress frame groaned in protest of his weight. He set aside his pile of photos and shuffled through the box for another in pained silence.

Glued to the floorboards, Andy was unable to look away as his eyes filled with unshed tears and his lips flattened into a rueful smile. This moment seemed so private, her presence almost certainly an infringement, but Uncle Dirk didn't seem to remember she was there.

So she looked down, stared at the photo still clutched in her fingers. The boy in it was nearly unrecognizable to her—his white-blond hair looked nothing like Uncle Dirk's walnut waves, and the freckles sprinkling his skin were nowhere to be found on the man before her, but somehow, something about that childish face screamed Dirk.

Without preamble, Uncle Dirk handed over another photo. When she took it gingerly, he stabbed a finger at it. "This kid here was an idiot. Didn't give two hoots about anybody but himself. There're a lot of things I'd do different if I'd known then what I know now."

Andy had to assume the photo was of him, but her breath caught when, for the breadth of a heartbeat, she thought she was looking at—no. It was impossible, and she knew it. She shook her head to clear the image. "This is you?"

He nodded.

The young man staring back at her looked carefree and

full of life, his face alight with sunshine, a lake peeking over his shoulder as he held out a hooked fish with triumph. Upon closer inspection, Andy could see who it was without doubt; the blond hair had darkened and the freckles were not so prominent, increasing the resemblance to Uncle Dirk greatly—especially since there was no denying that smile.

"That was taken not so long before I left here." Dirk tapped a corner of the photo. "I used to go with Pop to that lake every summer for whole weekends. We'd camp out under the stars and sing songs to his old guitar, catch our dinner and skin it ourselves, then cook it over an open fire. It was pure adventure…" His voice trailed into a broken sigh. Andy gave the photo back to him along with the others she still held. He stared at them with a glazed expression."It was the only thing we did together, just the two of us."

Andy knew the matter was sensitive, yet still she found herself pressing. "Was John a standoffish father?"

Dirk pulled a new stack of photographs from the box, breathing out loudly, but his demeanor remained calm and open. "Hmm. I guess some would say that. I think he just didn't know what to do with us. Besides, I was the only one he had anything in common with. He was an outdoorsman through and through. Ruthie hated the outdoors, and Larry was always working. Soon as he was old enough to have a lemonade stand, he became an enterprising kid; the day he turned eighteen, he already had a place to go." Dirk flexed his fingers again, letting them ripple one after the other back and forth against his palm. Andy noticed there was a nail missing from one pinky, and wondered vaguely how it had seen its demise. "Wasn't too far off from here, where he went, but it was enough. Instead of paying rent, he worked for a widower who let him stay in a bunk room in his barn. He did plumbing work with him for a couple years, then did odd jobs until he had what he lacked to buy himself a trailer house about thirty miles east. He's lived there ever since."

Andy surprised herself by saying aloud, "He could have seen them more."

Dirk lifted a brow.

"I, uh, just mean that thirty miles isn't so far…."

His responding chuckle was dark. "No, it ain't. I reckon it wasn't just me who could've learned a thing or two from Patsy about looking after our elders."

Andy waited for him to say more, but he was caught up in new photos. Her mind churned with twice as many questions as before, and she couldn't let the conversation die—but she didn't want to appear too eager. She reached into the box for more photos.

Many of these were of a teenage Dirk by himself—soaked from head-to-toe poolside, riding a bike with no hands, lounging in the grass on a picnic blanket making a funny face, hanging head-first out of a tree. But there were a few others scattered in between—him in his cap and gown surrounded by friends at graduation, poised on the back of a Harley behind a Santa Claus in sunglasses and a leather vest, looking dashing dressed in a tux holding the hand of a blurry-faced girl in pink lace—and he looked genuinely happy.

It confused Andy. Out of every question in her mind, the one she kept hearing over and over was due to the one thing she knew each of John and Betty's surviving children had in common: their resolve to leave their parents' house when they turned eighteen. Had John's limited attention really been so demoralizing?

Gathering her favorites from the stack, Andy swallowed and held them up to Uncle Dirk. "You looked so happy in these. Surely you had something of a fun childhood?"

He took the photos, his smile nostalgic but eyes still

somber. "There were plenty times I was happy. Times we all were, I guess. But no, I wouldn't say I had a fun childhood."

"Why is that?"

"Heh, gosh. Well. My parents weren't the most exciting people. They did the same dang things every day of their adult lives, barely changing at all. Went to the same places, ate the same meals, read the same newspaper and books and magazines, wore the same clothes. Larry always used to say they lived in a bubble, and it was like life didn't exist for them outside of it. They couldn't imagine life being any other way—just routine. Day after day, year after year." Dirk squeezed his brow bone, then shrugged with one shoulder. "I dunno. Some people run from their problems, and others cope by clinging to what they know with everything they got. My parents were clingers. When they started having kids, they didn't know how to fit us into their bubble. Ma clung to sewing and reading and flowers and stuff, and Pop turned to the outdoors. Us kids, we had to turn to other places, other people for a lot of stuff." He plucked out the snapshot of him in the tux with the girl, and something passed over his face that broke Andy's heart in half. His voice was barely audible when he muttered, "Like *you*, for one."

"An old girlfriend?" Something told Andy there was more to it than that.

"One of the things I'd do different."

The pain behind Dirk's eyes was almost enough to make Andy drop the whole thing, sensing it was the most painful subject for him yet, but she was too far in it now. "What happened?"

The cell phone on the window ledge pumped out a Michael Jackson ballad as the next moments passed in stillness, the only movement in the room being the occasional flutter of the curtains with the autumn breeze blowing in. Uncle Dirk concentrated on the girl in the photo, and Andy concentrated on him. For an agonizing while she thought he wouldn't reply to her question, but then he spoke in a shaky whisper.

"We let fear make our choices for us." A tear dripped onto the photo, and he blinked hard and fast as though awaking from a bad dream.

With no other warning, Uncle Dirk threw the photos on the bed, rising so fast from the mattress that he lost his balance and nearly fell over the rocking chair; the baseball bat Jacob had left behind clattered to the floor. "Sorry, Andy, but I—I can't do this. You can sort them if you want. I gotta...I gotta go."

Hands raking his hair like a man on the brink of madness, he fled from the room.

CHAPTER FIVE

THE STUDY HAD ONCE been a parlor; of that, Jacob was certain. It made the most sense with this floor plan, what with its Victorian design. There was also a hazy memory tickling Jacob's mind, of watching John haul out plush loungers and tea tables, returning with bookshelves and the desk. Why Jacob was there during that time was anyone's guess; probably his mother had dropped him off in one of her occasional seasons of husband-hunting that stirred up Jacob's life when Ruth was between marriages. He did recall, though, Ruth's being there at some point, because in the memory she had said the room looked too unsophisticated to be a "real study".

Even so, the room had gone from formal sitting room to practical home office in one day.

That had been before John's retirement, but the study was used more recently as another overflow space for clutter; although, Jacob was initially more pleased with this room than he'd been with anything all day. It had apparently been sealed off before the disaster of mass hoarding struck the house, so its disarray was minor in comparison. Still, he tried to picture it without its discolored damask wallpaper, the walls refreshed with a few coats of creamy paint in a warm, neutral shade, the moth-eaten curtains replaced with floor-length sheers like the ones Andy had been contemplating for the office in their would-be new apartment. His favorite part remained the original wooden floor, which he imagined buffed to such a shine that he could see his reflection in it.

He had to admit the house was a real treasure, underneath all the mess. Throughout the day, with each room he'd spent time in, he kept envisioning Andy in it, when it was theirs. For this room, the study, he saw her late at night on a Friday, after their typical movie date, hunched over this same oak desk. It was currently covered in dust, debris, and rat droppings, but in his vision, it was cleaned up and looking brand new, smelling of lemon furniture polish rather than decay.

That weird, modern-industrial lamp Andy loved so much (the one Jacob detested) was on in the corner, clashing stubbornly with the era of the room's architecture. Its light cast sharp shadows over her as she worked. She was comfortable, safe, wearing her favorite Beatles sweatshirt with the thumb holes she'd cut into the wrist cuffs, her paisley print glasses perched on her nose, as they were every night after she removed her contact lenses. With a determination that was equal parts aggravating and admirable, she flipped through paperwork that could've waited until Monday; and somewhere in the back of her mind, she noted how great it was to finally have a space other than the kitchen table to spread out when she brought her work home.

Yes. He could see them in this house. In its present state, it was a tough image to conjure without using your imagination, but luckily Jacob was good at that.

Dream later, focus now.

He disengaged from the daydream, going back to his self-appointed, low-key task of checking all the walls for possible secret passages or hidden compartments. It was an unlikely possibility he'd find either, but he was nothing if not thorough. He'd already gone through the drawers and the desktop, even given the bookcases a tedious once-over to ensure nothing was crammed in between the books. So far he'd turned up nothing.

His skin prickled with irritation. *They* have *to be here somewhere!*

The last wall was another bust. Clenching and unclenching his fists, he brushed the mounting panic aside and went about the routine of sorting the room's contents. Useless items went on one side of the room for disposal, stuff to sell or donate was in the center, and anything worth keeping went under the windows. His work was steady and methodic. As he sorted, he marveled again at the size of these rooms, at the whole house, wondering how it could seem even bigger to him as an adult than it did when he was a child. He usually experienced the opposite sensation.

A shrill beeping erupted from his pocket. He removed his gritty gloves to answer the call.

"Jacob Tamblyn, Harmeling Tree Services," he said in his gruff occupational voice. Although he was out of his twenties now, he still looked and sounded too young for anyone well-seasoned in his field, and he thought the deeper voice inspired clients to take him more seriously. Andy hated it, believed it made him pretentious, but he did it anyway.

"Hello, Jacob, it's Michael Marsden with Dewey and Hatch Law Associates. How are you?" Jacob recognized the unmistakable voice of his grandfather's lawyer. The older man's gravelly baritone put Jacob's attempts to shame; still, he kept the facade in place for the sake of his pride.

"Afternoon, sir. Doing fine. I'm at John and Betty's now."

"Oh? And how is everything?"

"The whole family is here, as dictated by the will."

"Wonderful news. That's actually why I called. I wanted to be assured everyone held up their end of the bargain."

"So far so good. It'll take more than a few days to clean up, though." Jacob thought of his mom as she'd gone outside to smoke cigarettes every few minutes. "I wouldn't go dispensing any funds yet. Certain people...may lose their motivation to help out."

Mr. Marsden conceded a snicker. "Indeed. When do you foresee the project to be completed in its first phase?"

Jacob scratched his head, mentally calculating. "I'd say a week? But everyone will need to go back to work, so I can't expect them to stay past the weekend."

"Understood." Mr. Marsden prattled off a short list of further instructions for Jacob and Andy in the coming weeks, then reminded Jacob to keep him apprised.

"Will do, Mr. Marsden. Thanks for the call."

He hung up, turning to see Ruth propped against the doorframe of the study.

"Having a chat with the negotiator of our hostage situation?" she questioned airily while fingering an errant strand of frosted blonde hair away from her eyes.

"Say what you want about the man, but he's only doing his job. Granddaddy made the rules; Marsden only enforces them. I thought I already asked you not to smoke inside?"

"You've hardly spoken a word to me all the day long," she said behind one of her condescending smiles. "Wanted to give you another reason." She took a long drag off the cigarette in her left hand. "It's almost done anyway."

"Put it out, or go outside. Those are your choices."

"Lord, Jake." Ruth's eyes rolled.

"Just do it, would you?"

As he moved over to the desk, Jacob caught her in the reflection of the glass doors on a curio cabinet ahead of him

—she mashed the glow of her cigarette against the doorframe next to her head, making smoky black holes in the wood. The stump fell to floor, and she stomped it with her heel.

Jacob released a hot breath through his nose but didn't comment.

"You sure got bossy since I seen you last."

Jacob's jaw worked in a stiff circle and he slid a tall pile of department store catalogues from the desktop into a trash bag. "Not bossy. Some people grow up and get smart. You should take a class on it sometime."

"Careful, son. Them's fighting words." Ruth sauntered into the room and heaved herself onto the desk. She promptly crossed her legs and took note of Jacob's sell/donate section. "Gonna try to sell this crap?" She coughed out an indignant laugh. "Waste of time, Jake. This house is packed with nothing but junk. You should light a match and let the place burn."

"Thanks for the input, but that's not what Granddaddy wanted. I'm doing it his way." *I owe him that, at least.*

Ruth shrugged as if he'd told her he didn't want mustard on his hot dog. "Suit yourself, kiddo. No skin off my nose once I get what's mine outta all this."

It took everything in Jacob not to slam his palms against the desk and roar at her. But she was his mother, that pesky flesh and blood, and although she was lousy company, he would do everything within his ability to keep his cool as long as they were working together. Besides, he wasn't the best candidate to be preaching at her anyway.

He did, however, say tersely, "Break's over, Ruthie. That living room won't clean itself."

"Would it kill you to call me 'Mom'? I did birth you. I figure I've earned at least that much respect from my only child."

Years of disappointment and animosity bubbling just

beneath the surface, Jacob said in a low, even voice, "Would it kill *you* to apply yourself? To do this *one* thing for your family?"

Ruth's eyes heated, her frown so deep it made her chin double up. "I took off of my busy schedule to be here for you and that—that...*wife* of yours, and I didn't have to do that. It was an act of kindness from a mother to her son, and you're spitting on it."

Jacob felt his ears catching fire, his lungs compressing in a way that squeezed all his breath into his throat. Every ounce of calm he'd so carefully preserved fell away in an instant. "What a load of malarkey you're selling! We all know the only reason you're here is because it's the one hoop between you and your inheritance. And if Marsden wasn't on stand-by just *waiting* for me to call and tell him you didn't show for clean-up, you'd have skipped out in a heartbeat! You'd already be on a plane to the Bahamas to celebrate your latest cash cow!"

Ruth's hands flew to her chest as though he'd struck her a physical blow. "For Pete's sake, Jacob! You can't talk down to me like I'm trash you picked up off this floor. It ain't right!"

"'Right'?! Since when do you care about what's 'right' for anyone but yourself? You're the single most self-centered person I've met in my life!"

"How *dare* you! I'm the least selfish person I know!" Her bottom lip wobbled.

"The wobbly lip bit? Seriously? I'm not nineteen anymore, Ruthie. Give me a little credit, huh?"

"You're treating me like this horrible burden you can't wait to be rid of. How is that supposed to make me feel?"

"How can you not know, somewhere inside you, that you *are* a burden?! You're either in denial, or you're finally so far gone inside your own lies and manipulations that you're devoid of all reason."

"I don't have to sit here and take this abuse. I didn't do a thing to deserve such an attack!"

"You're delusional!" Jacob could hardly stomach what he was hearing. It was classic Ruth, and no matter how many times she pulled these "victim" stunts, it never failed to poke at an already inflamed wound for Jacob. "This is exactly why I don't come around you anymore, Mom."

Ugh. He hadn't meant to call her that....

Hearing the term of endearment reverberating off his eardrums made him cringe internally. The urge to correct himself was strong, but what good would that do besides highlight the mistake to Ruth? He was usually so careful to call her "Ruth" or "Ruthie" to her face; the emotional distance of it was a source of meager protection for his battered heart, and it didn't hurt that her lip curled a little when he did it.

Though he need not have worried. Ruth was so absorbed in her performance of anguish that she'd missed it entirely, her focus turned to producing waterworks at full blast. "This is what I'm talking about!" she bawled, all sense of dignity abdicated. "You don't even care about me anymore—I'm just an extra pair of hands to clean up this *stupid* house. You're letting that gal'darn lawyer give you advice, roping us all into this mess so you can hold our own money over our heads!" She wailed and splayed her fingers over her face, gurgling and coughing, reaching out to steady herself on a chair. Andy would have called her a "hot mess"; Jacob thought it had never applied so absolutely. "Everyone treats me like d-dirt. I put on a st-strong f-face like it doesn't b-bother me, but it does."

Over her cries, Jacob noticed the rest of the house had gone still, utterly silent. He pulled at his hair, feeling his cheeks flood with heat. *This is the seventh grade science fair all over again.* His mother cherished an audience for her tirades and meltdowns; the bigger the better, but four people was more than enough.

"You're being dramatic," he growled.

This only made Ruth's squalling worse. She began to shake all over, forcing herself into a fit. "So insensitive towards me!" She shook her head at him as if she were seeing him as a monster for the first time. "What's happened to you, Jake? Did you plumb forget about all those years I raised you, put a roof over your head, clothes on your back, food in your belly? I put you through college, Jacob! You wouldn't have met Andrea without me, you wouldn't have that precious job of yours! But no, don't thank me, don't *appreciate* me for that!"

Face stained with tears, nose running, and mangled sobs choking out of her, the whole display was a marvel. She blubbered on some more, unintelligible, and if Jacob had been a few years younger, had less experience with these episodes, less of an understanding of her strategy to manipulate…he might fall for it. But he'd been through this too many times by now. For the first time in his life, he wouldn't let her play this maddening game she'd invented for no other reason than to get her way.

It had taken him years to figure it out, but eventually Jacob knew Ruth must have done this to his father, too—it had probably always worked for her. Until one day, the man left home and didn't come back. He'd chosen to abandon his family rather than stand up to his own wife because she'd beaten him so far down with her crushing *need*. It didn't make it right, what he'd done—Jacob had never forgiven his father for leaving—but he at least understood now. A person could only stand so much before they broke.

Jacob put up both hands, meeting Ruth's gaze with unwavering severity. "I'm done."

"What does *that* mean?"

"It means you can go, Ruth. I won't stop you."

She stared back with horror-stricken eyes, red-rimmed and framed by false lashes. "But...Jacob, what about—"

"Your money? Don't worry, I'll see that you get it. Just go."

"But the house...it ain't finished," she sniffed.

"No, it's not. But I don't care. I just want you gone."

"But Jake—"

"Stop. Don't talk, just leave." His face felt stiff, hardened into an impenetrable mask of ice. "And don't bother coming back."

CHAPTER SIX

"YOU OKAY?"

THE QUESTION was voiced by Uncle Dirk, but Jacob had seen it branded across every face he'd encountered in the last hour. Andy had come in earlier and rubbed his back in soothing circles, even given him a hug. When he'd looked at her at last, he saw her mouth opening and closing again and again, yet neither of them spoke. She'd left having said nothing at all. Later, and at different times, both uncles stood outside the door of the upstairs bedroom where Jacob had retreated to work in solitude after sending his mother away. Matching frowns marred the mens' expressions, their arms folded across their chests. Uncle Larry, same as Andy, said nothing—simply watched Jacob work, at last scratching his bald spot and lumbering away as though unsure how he'd ended up there.

Uncle Dirk, though, hadn't gone anywhere.

Not knowing what to say in response to his question, Jacob kicked an empty box from his walking path as he carried another, full of collectible toys, to the sell/donate section of this room. "I'll get over it," he answered finally.

Uncle Dirk scuffed his boot into the floorboards. "Sorry she yelled at you. She's painful good at that."

Jacob's chest clenched up at the memory of what had transpired. His hands fumbled the box as he made to set it down, and several toy jacks escaped to the floor. As he crouched to retrieve them, he grumbled, "Nothing I haven't gotten from her a billion times before."

Uncle Dirk's sigh came all the way from the bottom of his lungs as he pinched the bridge of his nose. His voice was exhausted and far away as he murmured, "Sometimes parents are so much better at making mistakes than they are at being parents."

The jacks were safely back in their box, and Jacob had the sudden urge to sit. There was a straight-backed chair near the window, and he slid into it. He stayed still for a long time, and so did Uncle Dirk; apparently he was equally satisfied to keep the silence between them.

Jacob could hear the music of Andy's light footfalls down the hall, answered back and forth by the dense clunks of Uncle Larry's in the living room. The sunlight filtering in from the newly-exposed window fell in golden streaks across everything, but dark shadows remained in contrast on the underside of all that was lit up so brightly.

He licked his lips, tasting dust. "When I was growing up, I didn't understand why my dad worked so much. I thought maybe it was because of me, because I always wanted him to spend every moment with me when he was home. I would beg and beg, crawl all over him when he just wanted to sit down at the table and eat a meal in peace. Some days I'd even grab onto his leg and not let go until he played with me."

A squirrel bobbed across the windowsill outside, stopping momentarily to look at Jacob with black, hollow eyes before it scampered off.

"I didn't start putting two and two together until after the divorce, when I stayed weekends with him. He was so much happier—he didn't have a new woman, so I knew it wasn't that. He had the same job he'd always had, made the same money, had the same friends and hobbies. Then I realized what had been keeping him away all that time: her."

"I know, son."

Jacob lifted his eyes, seeking out Uncle Dirk's, and the bleakness there so reflected his heart that, for the moment, he found solace in that another human being wasn't merely being sympathetic, but knew precisely what he felt.

Uncle Dirk sat on the bed near Jacob's chair. Dust unfurled around them in opaque clouds that shot up Jacob's nose, but he couldn't find it in himself to care. "Jake," said Uncle Dirk, "there're two kinds of people in this world. The kind that run and hide when things get tough, and the kind that bury themselves in something familiar that they can control. Everybody's one or the other 'til they learn to face their demons head-on. Your momma was the latter, and your daddy the former. Ruthie tried to control Harrison, and it pushed him further and further away 'til all she had left was you." He deliberated, raking his gaze across the room as if memories were leaking out of the walls at the seams. Then he shook his head, eyes sliding shut. "But in the beginning, before things were tough, Jake...they were okay together."

There was a short chirp of laughter from Jacob. "I find that hard to believe."

"Kid, when's the last time you saw your momma around people she wasn't related to?"

Jacob clasped his hands over each of his knees. "I...don't know. It's been awhile."

"Well, your momma hides her crazy when it benefits her. Harrison didn't have a clue what he'd gotten himself into, I reckon. By the time he saw the writing on the wall, I guess he decided it was worth sticking it out best he could, for your sake. Maybe he thought he'd last longer, I dunno. But I know he tried." Jacob gave him a sharp look, and Dirk doubled back. "Hey, I'm not saying he wasn't wrong to jet off. But the man's human, son. Anyway. What I mean to say is that Ruthie...she's always been awful good at pretending when she wants to be, and she pretended to be normal when she met your daddy. Probably helped that only a handful of people knew about her condition, and—"

Jacob's head snapped up. "Wh-What? Her condition?"

Uncle Dirk's thick brows darted towards his hairline. At first he was speechless, then a cloud passed over his face. "This family, I *swear*..." He ran a hand through the tangled waves of his hair and smacked his lips. "I take it you didn't know."

"I *still* don't know—I have no idea what you're talking about."

"Listen, kid. There's no easy way to say this...shoot, I sure never thought I'd be the one to tell you, but you need to know." Dirk's hands fell to his lap where they wrung one another back and forth in a reluctant confrontation. "Okay, I'm just gonna say it." Contrarily, his lips locked together, eyebrows drawn in conjunction with his scowl. Everything in the room became something to fixate on, his eyes slipping over Jacob repeatedly without stopping.

"Uncle Dirk..." Jacob didn't have the patience for qualms; he just wanted to know what was going on.

After a long lull, his uncle cleared his throat but didn't raise his eyes. "Jake," he said in a coarse whisper, "your momma...well, she was...she *is* sick."

A slow thrumming filled Jacob's ears. "Sick?"

"Yeah. In here, though." Dirk tapped his temple. "Ruthie was diagnosed with a slew of mental disorders by the time she was sixteen."

Numbness trickled through Jacob's body, starting in his

chest and rolling through his limbs to the very tips of his fingers and toes. A metallic taste seeped across his tongue. It took several false starts before he choked out, "What disorders?"

"The main problem was narcissistic personality disorder, but she also had manic depression with psychopathic tendencies, and there was talk of her being psychotic."

"As in...hallucinations?"

"Delusional beliefs."

The musty smell of the room was suddenly more than Jacob could bear. He jumped up, the force of his legs against the chair knocking it over. He fought to open the window behind him, nails scratching up paint as he struggled with the latch. It took Uncle Dirk's quiet assistance before the pane swung open on its rusty hinges. Thrusting his head out, he gulped the fresh air greedily, head spinning so fast his vision blurred.

Apparitions of Ruth's face swarmed his mind—the way she smiled wanly and said he "hadn't got her brains" when he'd cobbled together a homely birdhouse made of wood scraps when he was six. The way she threw her head back in an incredulous laugh when he'd showed her a certificate from school that declared him "most likely to become an astronaut". The curl of her lip when he bought carnations on her birthday instead of roses, even though he'd saved up his lunch money for two weeks to buy them. The crinkle of her nose when he introduced her to Jade Crenshaw, his date to the junior prom, and how she'd smiled without showing her teeth when she said to Jade, "Don't get too attached to him, missy. *Your* babies would be dogs, and I won't be having ugly grandkids."

Dirk's voice was soft. "Sorry, Jake. I always figured you knew."

...the way she gritted her teeth and flared her nostrils the first time he'd had the guts to call her insane. She'd slapped him, her eyes flashing as she hissed, "You ever call me that again, son, and I'll wipe that smart look off your face for good."

The way she'd absolutely meant it.

"Is any of that hereditary?"

Uncle Dirk gave him a quizzical look. "Possibly. I'm no expert, though. You should ask a doctor."

Jacob's face was being stabbed with a hundred needles, and all he could do was stand there at the window, half out and half in, trying to steady his breath. "Thank you...for telling me."

"I oughta leave you to get your head straight. I'll, uh, start on the room next door." Jacob heard Dirk's footsteps recede to the doorway, but then he stopped. "Should I send Andy in?"

Jacob's voice was almost inaudible. "No."

The door closed behind Dirk with a click. "I'd leave him be, kiddo. He needs to be alone for a bit."

Andy was hunched against the wall in the hallway; a dust rag hung limply in one hand, a can of air freshener in the other. "I don't believe this."

Dirk frowned. "How much did you hear?"

A tear coursed down her cheek, leaving a track of pinker skin as it plowed through dirt and grime toward her jawline. She was shaking. "More than I've heard in seven years."

CHAPTER SEVEN

JACOB PACED A LINE of flattened weeds in the overgrown backyard for half an hour before he could convince himself to make the call. The whole time the line rang, he debated hanging up; but then he'd probably get a return call, so he'd wind up in the same dilemma.

Someone picked up on the other end, and a man said, "Hello? Jake?"

"Why didn't you tell me?"

Several seconds ticked by before the voice asked uncertainly, "What do you mean?"

"Don't pull that crap with me, Dad. I'm thirty years old, isn't it time people stopped hiding stuff from me? I want the truth. Why. Didn't. You *tell* me?"

Harrison Tamblyn said nothing for a long time—too long.

"Dad, please. I'm begging you. I just wanna know why."

"Jake," Harrison began with a sigh, "she's your mom. And as much as she *can* love, she loves you, needs you. I couldn't—I didn't want to—" He stopped and collected himself. "I didn't want you to know because you would see her differently. Even if you didn't mean for it to happen, she would've become a diagnosis to you."

"No, she wouldn't—"

"Yes, son, she would've. You were always looking for a way to label her, figure out why she is the way she is."

Jacob chewed the inside of his cheek, trying not to cry. "Dad, we could've helped her. Why wasn't she seeing doctors, going to therapy, taking medicine—*something?!*"

"I tried that when I found out, son. She has never accepted her diagnoses, doesn't want to admit there's anything wrong with her."

"But maybe if I—"

"It won't help, Jake. I'm sorry."

Jacob could feel his control slipping, his hands beginning to shake. "You're telling me there's *nothing* anyone can do for her?"

"Nothing short of changing her mind about seeking help."

"What if I talked to her?"

"She won't listen, but see for yourself if you have to. I don't blame you if you can't take my word for it." Harrison sighed again. "But I've been down this road, Jake—it's not pretty. I wanted to spare you, and you can hate me for it, but if you keep on like this...."

"What? *What*, Dad?"

"It *will* make things worse."

A biting wind caught Jacob under the arms and pushed him backward, licking the edges of his flannel shirt and stinging his sides where the fabric flapped hard against him. "So I should just give up. Not even try?"

Harrison released an exasperated groan. "Jacob, it is what it is. You can accept it, or you can spend the rest of your life beating your head against a wall trying to change what can't be changed. It's your choice."

Jacob had thought his heart couldn't break any further,

but clearly he'd been wrong. He breathed out so long his lungs began to ache. "Gotta go, Dad."

"Jake—"

He hung up and stuffed the phone into his pocket. With a guttural cry, he kicked up weeds and cursed the sky until every muscle in his legs screamed for rest. He dropped to his knees and cried until his tear ducts were emptied, and all he felt was a pit in his stomach.

CHAPTER EIGHT

IT TOOK EVERY GRANULE of Andy's concentration not to be furious at Jacob. It was unrighteous anger, too, which made her doubly agitated—but for a moment, she didn't want to care about that.

She'd been asking him questions about his family life for seven years. It was always a fight to pry even a smidgen of information out of him; he was the master of vague answers, and he wasn't a long-winded guy anyway, even when he did want to talk. Pressing him had never been rewarding.

She blew air from her nostrils as she wiped down books from Patsy's old bookcase and threw them one by one into a box harder than necessary. There was a forceful thunk with every new addition.

When would he open up to her about his innermost thoughts and feelings? She was his best friend, his confidante, his wife, for crying out loud! Shouldn't he feel free to discuss anything with her? It was bad enough when they were only dating, but four years into marriage? Why keep secrets, no matter how small?

A hostile snarl welled up behind her ribcage. Her teeth ground together as she worked to stifle it.

It was becoming more and more clear to her that it wasn't as simple as "they embarrass me" and "we just aren't close like your family", the excuses she'd gotten from him many times before. Why wouldn't he give her more? She didn't hide anything from him; it wasn't fair to be kept in the dark like this when she was so forthcoming.

Maybe she should start coming up with some secrets of her own!

Stop it, Andy, came the voice of reason, making her pause mid-wipe with her cloth poised on the binding of a velvety hardback. *Your husband is hurting right now—think of him, not yourself.* She screwed up her face, enough shame flooding through her that she had half a mind to punish herself with a list of all the horrible things she deserved for being so heartless.

"Hey again."

Startled, Andy whirled to see Uncle Dirk entering the bedroom, hands in his pockets, expression forlorn.

"Sorry to throw off your momentum, but I, uh, changed my mind...." He walked to the edge of the bed, looking down at all the photos still lying where he'd left them earlier. Andy hadn't had the emotional capacity to sort them yet, and figured it was probably a project best suited for when she needed to take a load off her feet.

It took effort to keep her voice casual, her mood so often too obvious. "What about?"

Uncle Dirk didn't answer, but stood still for what felt like an eternity, his only movement being his eyes searching the mattress inch by inch. Andy went quietly back to her task, leaving him to his thoughts—but at long last, he reached out as if in slow motion and plucked just one photo from the bed.

She couldn't see which one it was, but she had a guess.

He held it with gentle fingers in both hands, focus intense as he soaked it in. When he finally cleared his throat and looked up at Andy, she was back in her own little world.

Dirk had expected to owe her an explanation, but she appeared content in leaving him to his own devices. Thankful for that, he slipped the photo into his back pocket and tip-toed out, his mind already submersed deep in the ocean of a past life.

CHAPTER NINE

"I WANT TO KNOW everything."

Dirk turned to see Jacob hovering in the doorway to the bedroom he was cleaning, their roles from earlier reversed. His nephew wore the wizened face of a much older man, drawing a deep breath out of Dirk. He tipped his head toward Jacob as he asked "Like what?" then went back to stuffing old newspaper into a trash bag.

"Everything," Jacob said again, "whatever you know. And Uncle Dirk," he said pointedly, waiting until his uncle met his gaze, "don't spare me."

Dirk rolled his shoulders and stretched a long moment before saying blandly, "Okay." He tied off the trash bag and hunted for a fresh one as he gestured toward the bed. "Have a seat."

He didn't have to tell Jacob twice. Like a young child awaiting a campfire story, Jacob's eyes were round saucers in his head as he sat down and folded his hands over his thighs. "*Everything*, Uncle Dirk," he persisted.

"Yeah, yeah, I heard you the first time, kid," Dirk chuckled. He picked up where he'd left off with the new trash bag.

"And just so we're clear, I don't know a heck of a lot, you get me?"

Jacob nodded.

"Okay, then. Where you want me to start?"

"Childhood. Anything relevant you can remember."

"Hmm. Well. It was a long time ago...."

"Okay."

Uncle Dirk straightened from his work and scratched his chin, and Jacob wished impatiently that he would not waste another second. He was on pins and needles when Dirk began, "As a kid, Ruthie was...off. Everybody could see it, but it was hard to tell what the problem was, something you couldn't quite nail down, you know? As she got older, she was meaner, aggressive, and always jealous of Patsy; she didn't care for it when people paid attention to her instead of Ruthie. Wanted to hear people sing her praises a lot—if she made a C on a test, you'd have thought that was worthy of a gold star. She wanted everybody to swoon and tell her how smart she was and stuff. It was a strange mix of being insecure and being high on herself."

This was odd to Jacob, having someone give an account of his mom this way. He'd grown so accustomed to avoiding any mention of her that doing the opposite felt foreign. "That's a little too familiar."

"Yep. Drove a big wedge between her and...well, everyone, really. Outside of the family, though, she had this way of pretending. It was a real good act; could've convinced me sometimes. She knew how to draw people in, so she made lots of friends through the years. But it never failed—once she reached a certain point in knowing someone, she'd let out the crazy."

Jacob stared hard at the tips of his shoes where there was still caked dirt and green debris from his violent foray outside. "You said before that she was diagnosed by sixteen?"

"Right. I don't know all the details, mind you, but after Ruthie hit puberty, she really lost control. Mood swings like the dickens, screaming and yelling all the time over nothing, big time manipulative behaviors, and other stuff that scared Ma and Pop. But back then, any kind of mental instability was something to be ashamed of. People kept that kinda thing under wraps, so it was a private struggle for our family. None of us talked about it outside the house; even inside it, we rarely mentioned it. Made Ma upset. Though, it was our biggest point of contention, for all of us. We lived with it daily but never felt okay discussing it, even after doctors got involved and there were tests done and medications prescribed. Again, don't know the details, but I do know Ruthie wasn't letting herself be treated. I saw her on more than one occasion flushing pills down the toilet, then later telling Ma she took them."

"Didn't you tell your mom? You didn't let her get away with that, did you?"

Dirk's mouth became a flat line for a moment, then he said stoutly, "I did...the first few times. Ruthie wanted to kill me; tried to traumatize me, too. Let out Larry's old pet snake he'd passed down to her when he moved out. I woke up with it wrapped around my neck one night. She swore up and down she ain't had nothing to do with it, but I know she did. That thing couldn't have gotten out on its own." He shivered. "Still can't stand snakes."

"Geez."

"Yeah, she was—is—a real piece of work."

Swallowing hard, Jacob asked, "So what did they do? About the medicine?"

"Forced it on her awhile. Ma would stand there like a

guard dog and watch, check under her tongue and all that. It worked for a long time." He sighed, and when he spoke again he could no longer stave off the edge.

"Then she got herself a boyfriend. She'd had boyfriends before, but not like this. She was obsessed with the guy, Terry, Tommy, Timmy—I forget." He waved a dismissive hand and went on, "Ruthie wanted the whole nine yards with him. Then he broke up with her to go out with some other girl who was putting out. Tore Ruthie up so bad she holed up in her room for days—only came out when Pop threatened to whip her backside for being so dang belligerent. After that she started throwing tantrums about her meds again. Ma took her back to the doctor and I don't know what happened, but I never saw or heard of any more meds."

Jacob chewed on that information. "The doctor stopped prescribing them."

"That's my guess. Probably wanted to give something else a try, something she'd be more compliant with. But whatever it was, it didn't do much good. Her...*symptoms* got worse and worse. She was the main reason Larry had left home so fast, and by the time she was old enough to leave, she did, too. No one to coerce her back to the doctor. No one to keep her accountable."

"How did she survive on her own?" The question knotted up Jacob's insides as he thought of every horrifying potential answer.

"She was resourceful. Remember, she was good at pretending with most folks. She got a job at a plant nursery in town, wormed her way into the hearts of the old couple that owned it; they didn't have kids of their own, so they treated her like the daughter they never had. Pretty sure they were also her benefactors in paying her way through the college courses she took. She never finished, though, because...uh, well...." He dropped off, eyeing Jacob awkwardly.

"What?"

"She met your daddy."

Jacob looked at his lap. "Ah."

"You sure you wanna know the rest, kid?"

Jacob didn't hesitate. "Yes. I—I need to."

Uncle Dirk wiped absently across his mouth and exhaled in a loud gust. "Well. From what I understand, she got all moony over him fast, like she had with that other guy Tony, or whatever it was. Guess your daddy helped her get her groove back. He came from money, had a little status she could mooch off of, and he opened her up to a whole new world with his upper crust society scene. She got hooked on the lifestyle, and it became like a god to her; pretty normal for somebody with narcissistic personality disorder.

"Harrison got her a job in an office owned by somebody in his fancy circle, and she thought she was the darndest thing since sliced bread. But then they got married, and she made it clear she had no inkling to work anymore. Found a special talent for spending Harrison's money, but I think he kinda expected to get a wife like that. That balance worked for them, for several years. I'd even go so far as to say they were happy...but then she had you, Jake." He shook his head sadly. "It was like somebody wrenched open all the loony parts inside of her and blew, spreading it like dandelion fluff. She was eaten up with it."

"I've heard my dad say something like that," Jacob remembered. "He used to tell me she changed after I was born. But how would *you* know that? You weren't around her back then any more than you are now." He glared suspiciously at his uncle.

Dirk's forehead creased. "Look, don't get smart; I'm trying to help here."

"Sorry." Abruptly, Jacob felt abashed, and he shook his head from side to side as though to dislodge any more bad reflexes.

"Despite what you may think, your daddy really loved your momma, even with all that craziness oozing out her ears. He called me a few times when you were little, asked me questions about her and our family. I don't know who else he must've talked with, but at some point when he called me again, he'd found out about her condition. He shared some things with me—not a lot, so don't get your hopes up—but the gist was that Ruthie got postpartum real bad, and she was never the same after. I think your daddy tried convincing her to get help, but she wouldn't. Things escalated up and up 'til she was mad as a hatter, and...."

"*What*, Uncle Dirk? Don't spare me, remember?"

Dirk tensed. "You sure?"

"Positive."

He sighed. "Your momma, Jake...she started...having affairs."

Jacob became very still. His blood was turning to ice in his veins.

"Still want me to go on?"

"Yeah." Although he meant it, Jacob's voice sounded weaker now.

If Uncle Dirk heard it, though, he chose to ignore it. He went on stiffly, "Between that and the crazy, after eight years...Harrison couldn't do it anymore. He was worried about separating you from her, though; that's why he never fought her for full custody."

"Dad never told me that...about the affairs."

"I'd imagine not."

"I overheard gossip, when she was married to Stan and again with Gary, but the rumor mill had never treated my mom well anyway, so I just assumed...."

"Understandable."

With a flick of his wrist, Jacob cracked his knuckles on one hand, then the other. Even with all the emotions swirling dangerously inside him, words stopped coming—he felt the need to *move*, any way and every way. He bolted upward off the bed, shaking out his hands and trudging up and down the length of the room on the working path Uncle Dirk had cleared in the mess. His grungy Chuck Taylors slapped out an angry rhythm on the wooden floor as he paced.

"After Mom and Dad divorced, I spent every weekend begging Dad to let me stay with him longer, and he wouldn't. Ever."

"He didn't want to take you from your momma, Jake. It would've done more harm than good."

Jacob's eyes burned when he turned them on Dirk. "For who? Me? Her? Or *him?*"

"All of you" was his uncle's gentle reply.

"I just don't understand how any father could let his kid go like that. It's wrong, irresponsible—it's selfish." He spat the last word out as if it were poisonous. "He knew I wasn't happy with her. He didn't want to give up being a bachelor again, that's all it was. The rest was an excuse given at *my* expense!" He jabbed a thumb into his chest, teeth gnashing as he fumed.

Uncle Dirk sat quietly for a long time, listening and watching, the color slowly draining from his face. When Jacob collapsed onto the bed again, out of breath, he leaned back slightly as he took in the change.

"Sorry. I sound like a ten-year-old, I know. Some jaded kid who can't get a grip on his mommy and daddy issues."

Uncle Dirk flexed his jaw. He reached into his back pocket, and his hand came back with a photo that was a little bent up around the edges; he hurriedly turned it face down over his lap so Jacob was unable to see what it was.

"Jake," he began in a strained voice, "I realize your daddy and me aren't the same guy. His reasons for things don't always line up with mine, and vice versa. But we have one sure thing in common."

Suddenly Jacob heard everything he'd been saying the last few minutes with new ears; he immediately felt heat rising all the way up his body.

"Oh man, Uncle Dirk, I-I'm sorry. That was a jerk move—on my part, *my* part," he rushed to clarify. He covered his eyes with one hand. "I'm an idiot."

"Not that I ain't getting a little kick out of listening to you beat yourself up," Uncle Dirk snickered, "but I mean to tell you something important. Care to listen?"

Without speaking, Jacob sucked in both lips and nodded fervently, feeling more foolish than he had in a long time.

Uncle Dirk turned his head to the side and stared out the window. His chest expanded and retracted again and again beneath his red plaid work shirt. "Most people got regrets by the time they get to be my age, your daddy's age—and we ain't no exception. I can't speak for Harrison, but I can tell you I got two regrets myself. They haunt me every single day." His eyes shifted to the photo in his lap, still facing down.

"One of them was letting go of a girl. The other was letting go of her child…our child." His Adam's apple bobbed as he gulped, grimacing as though the action hurt. "Sometimes it feels like it happened yesterday—but we were young, reckless, plain stupid. Especially me." Tears shimmered in his eyes. He pressed a restless hand to his forehead before it dropped and settled on his chin, mostly covering his mouth, then he used his other hand to flip over the photo.

He held it up to Jacob, who stared with widening eyes as his mind grappled with what he was seeing.

"Who is this…?" His heart pumped boisterously inside

him as if it would explode. He felt as though he'd swallowed his tongue, but his attention stayed trained on the photo before him.

Could it be?

"Sarah Marie Whistler." It sounded reverent the way every syllable melted over Uncle Dirk's lips, yet at the same time, his jaw seemed to trip over the last name as though rusty at saying it.

"You—you dated her?" Jacob's mouth wanted to trip over things, too. His world felt like it was tipping on its axis, bringing him with it. His skeleton seemed to liquify, his muscles useless as his frame went limp. Sitting up straight was more than he could contend with, so he slouched over, knees on his elbows to keep his position secure.

Uncle Dirk didn't notice. He replied, "'Ruined her life' is more like it. Got her in more trouble than a girl like that deserves to be in." He let out a small laugh without humor. "It was my fault it happened in the first place. She wanted us to get married out of high school, live downtown in a flat, have babies. In that order, like we was supposed to. But I couldn't wait." His head tilted forward heavily as if his neck gave out, and his voice grew raspy. "Sarah Marie's daddy was a banker. Nice man, respectable—'til the night he overheard her on the phone crying to her best friend.

"He lost it, whipped the tar out of her, then he walked all the way here and gave me everything he had left. Took Pop intervening to get him to quit, and that was after Pop got in a few good licks of his own. Mr. Whistler spent the night in jail, and the next thing I knew, he picked up the family and took off."

Jacob's mouth worked silently, but he couldn't get out the words running through his mind over and over. *There's no way. The likelihood...!*

"Weeks down the road, I had a letter from Sarah Marie

telling me she planned to keep the baby, but neither of them could have anything to do with me. There wasn't no return address and the postal markings weren't legible. None of her friends would tell me where they'd gone in fear of their own daddies; they wasn't supposed to have anything to do with me either, see." He leaned back and stared at the ceiling a minute, composing himself before continuing, "I did everything I could think of to try and track her down, but no one would help me. Eventually I graduated, and by then enough time had passed that I knew she must've had the baby. On my eighteenth birthday, I got together all my savings, packed my bags, hopped the bus, and started a physical search."

Jacob sat up straighter. Blood rushed in his eardrums, and the fringes of his vision seemed to ripple like water. He began doing calculations in his head.

Eighteenth birthday. *It fit!* Could it really be possible?

"I went to every town within a hundred miles that summer. I bussed tables and washed dishes in exchange for meals, slept under stairs, bathed in public locker rooms, scrubbed my clothes in the sink, and played Pop's old guitar on the street to earn bus fare to the next stop. I burned through phone books and used libraries to search public records looking for any trace of Sarah Marie's family, and when that didn't work, I checked church directories and sometimes even went door to door in smaller neighborhoods. It all got me nowhere." Uncle Dirk's face hardened. "All people saw when I came around asking questions was some vagrant creep who didn't have any business looking for this young woman, or else he'd know where to find her. In the end, I knew I'd exhausted my options. I couldn't very well search the entire country on foot, so I gave up and came home. Just like that."

Shocked mute, Jacob stared at him. There was a stretch of silence before he had enough presence of mind to realize he should say something. He prayed his voice would give nothing away. "Um. No one could blame you. I bet Sarah Marie—" He stopped. He didn't know what Sarah Marie would have thought, would have done had she known; he didn't know Sarah Marie at all, that much was obvious by this story. He cleared his throat. "What happened after that?"

"Well. Seeing how I was labeled no-good to the community now, I was worried about making life difficult for Ma and Pop, so I found work at a factory a few towns over and moved in the quarters they reserved for unmarried workers. Years later, Ma and Pop forwarded a letter from Sarah Marie. I must've been twenty-seven by then, still unattached. I'd tried dating at times, but it always left me with this…aching sense of loss. It ate at me from the inside out 'til I couldn't take it; I always went back to being alone. So there I was, at the same factory I'd been at since I was eighteen, barely a friend to speak of, and here came this letter from my missing sweetheart."

Jacob's fingers tightened over the edge of the mattress on either side of his legs. "What did she want?" he asked hoarsely. *The moment of truth….* He fought to keep from shaking, fear tearing at him with its claws.

"She'd heard from a high school friend of hers what I'd done the summer after graduation. She wanted to give me a chance to meet my kid. She gave me an address in Mississippi, told me when to come, and said they'd be expecting me."

"Mississippi?" Confusion coursed through Jacob, freezing his mind. Mississippi didn't make sense.

Uncle Dirk dipped his head again and nodded, regret contorting his features so completely it silenced the smattering of questions that had been building in Jacob's throat.

"I went. When I got there, I saw them on the swings together, and it hit me like a prize bull. There was my kid—my son, ten-years-old by then—and my Sarah Marie, the only woman I'd ever loved, beautiful as the day I met her."

Jacob's breath came out in a gust so fast it nearly choked him. *Oh, wow...this could really be happening!*

Uncle Dirk went on, totally unaware, his face burning red. "I'd been waiting for an opportunity like that since I was seventeen. And then I did the unthinkable, Jake—the lowest, crummiest thing I could've done. I turned tail and ran. I didn't look back, either. Like a pitiful coward, I drove all the way home, only stopping for gas." Dirk raked his fingers miserably through his hair, eyes screwed shut against the memory, jaw clenched so hard it quivered. He gulped in air between his teeth. "I never heard from Sarah Marie again. Fifty-three-years old and I don't know my own son's name. I doubt I ever will." Eyes still shut, he added feebly, "But you know, I made my bed, and I've been laying in it all these years like I deserve. I suspect your daddy does the same thing, Jake. Every blasted day. Both of us too busy hating ourselves to get up and change things. Hell-bent on being punished for those old mistakes, I guess."

The story finally over, Jacob clung to the mattress, too stunned to speak. His stomach turned with the after-effects of a shaken cocktail made up of shock, terror, solace, and uncertainty. For more than a minute, neither man made a peep. When Jacob found his voice again, it sounded dry and dead.

"Uncle Dirk, I'm so sorry."

A single tear made its way past his uncle's defenses; he wiped it away with the back of his hand. "Yeah. You and me both, kid."

The room pressed in around them, each of them rehashing and processing in their own way. But there was one question Jacob couldn't leave this spot without asking, no matter how insensitive it may seem.

Eyes on his hands, now in his lap, he positioned his face so he could see Uncle Dirk's expression in his peripheral. "Do you...ever think of...trying to find them? Now?"

The question generated no friction, Uncle Dirk's face bearing little change; Jacob thought it almost looked more bleak, although that seemed impossible. His answer came in a simple two words: "Not anymore."

CHAPTER TEN

"DIRK, HEY, IT'S PRAYTOR. Sorry I'm so late getting back to you. I was still following up on that lead in Detroit and was optimistic I'd have some good news, but-tuh…" The recording of Ryan Praytor sighed resolutely in Dirk's ear. "I'm sorry—it was another dead end." A moment of uneasy quiet. "I'm really sorry, Dirk. I genuinely thought we'd have some answers for you by now, but this does happen sometimes. We'll keep trying. Something will turn up." He cleared his throat. "Well. Uh, gimme me a call back if you have questions. Talk soon." The recording ended, and Dirk's arm fell away from his ear, cell phone still gripped firmly in his palm.

The voice message was old, from six days ago. Dirk hadn't made up his mind about what he would say to Praytor when he returned the call—that is, not until the conversation with Jacob about Sarah Marie and her son—his son. Dirk had known for the better part of a month that it was time to let go, yet he'd been holding onto one last strain of hope ever since Praytor had hit a promising lead that sent him up north for the first time. Maybe, just *maybe*…this time would be different.

But then he didn't hear from Praytor for longer than usual, and he didn't know what that meant. Dirk called him hoping for an update but had gotten only the PI's voicemail. It had taken Praytor three more days before he'd finally called back, and Dirk had missed the call in the shower.

He'd listened to the voice message dozens of times since, teetering on the edge between keeping up the search and calling it quits. He could no longer deny it was taking its toll on him to have such hope floundering in his chest, only to be let down again and again. For two and half years he'd been riding this roller coaster. If Praytor hadn't found Sarah Marie by now, he probably never would, and Dirk knew there could be no more rejecting that reality—or else losing his mind could become a very real possibility.

A steady wind whistled against the windows as Dirk sat in his car, the late afternoon light bending over the top of his old Mustang and grazing his lower body in the driver's seat. He'd been sent on an errand for more trash bags, water bottles, and cleaning supplies that weren't expired or otherwise questionable. He hadn't been able to stop thinking of what he and Jacob had talked about, and Jacob's resounding question: *Do you ever think of trying to find them? Now?*

"Not anymore," he whispered at the steering wheel.

With a resolve that surprised as much as encouraged him, Dirk selected the PI's number in his phone before bringing it back to his ear. The line rang until voicemail picked up. *Probably easier this way*, he thought. The tone at the end of the greeting sounded, and he cleared his throat.

"Hey Praytor, it's Dirk. Calling you back. Took me awhile, too, I know. Sorry. And no, it wasn't payback, I just..." He watched a vibrantly orange leaf fall onto his windshield. On the other side of it, Dirk saw a pretty woman holding the hand of a smiling little boy, the pair crossing the street towards a playground nearby. He took a quivering breath and plunged forward. "I had to make a decision, and it wasn't an easy one." The little boy stared up into the woman's face and grinned. She made a quirky face back at him, making them both laugh. "I've been thinking about it, a lot. I wasn't sure at first, but now...I think it's for the best."

The duo made it to the other side of the street, and the woman launched the boy into the air, each of them giggling, as she held his hands in hers and helped him onto the sidewalk. The boy went only a few steps before he turned and raised his arms to her in a different way, fingers grasping; she picked him up and settled him on her hip as they approached the playground. The little boy nestled his head on her shoulder and wrapped one arm around her neck, twirling her hair around his tiny hands.

Dirk lowered his eyes to the dashboard.

"I'm sorry, Praytor. I know you've been doing your best all this time, and I appreciate the work you've put into it for me, but I've decided...to put the investigation on hold." His throat pinched a little, but he didn't let it stop him. "Maybe indefinitely, I don't know. I need a break from this. Thanks for everything, man. I'll call you when...if...well. I'll call you."

As he hung up, he caught sight of the woman and child making themselves at home on the swings.

CHAPTER ELEVEN

IS THERE A NAME for this feeling?

Jacob had been asking himself that question for nearly an hour.

At one time there was an app on his phone that sent him words of the day, unique ones most people wouldn't hear in their lifetime, many of which identified feelings he wouldn't have guessed there ever existed a name for. The concept of naming certain sensations in life had fascinated him anomalously since then, but he hadn't felt so strong a need to name one himself until now.

Dirk's revelations to him had punched a hole in his perception of his family. He'd always known they harbored many secrets and private heartaches, but his wildest imagination was not creative enough to have concocted today's findings, not even if he'd had a million years to fabricate it all.

Corey, his brother-in-law, was the long-lost son of Jacob's uncle. That made Corey his cousin, which was….

Oh, how he wished for a word to describe it.

The closest he could get were 'stunned' and 'troubled'.

93

He longed to tell his wife, but no—it would be a mistake to tell her. Maybe someday, but…definitely not yet.

It was then that Jacob remembered the journal. He'd taken it to the car that morning, hidden it under the seat.

Already outside, sitting on the brick-laid border of his grandmother's wilted flower beds now overgrown with weeds, he rose and walked to the driveway. When the journal was once more in hand, he skirted the side of the house to the backyard, where he sat in a rusted metal chair half-hidden by the burn pile. No one was likely to bother him out here.

He smoothed a hand down the leather cover then flipped it open, instantly recognizing his grandmother's handwriting from the yearly birthday cards she used to send him. Andy was right—she had chronicled her slow crawl toward death. He didn't want to be hindered by it, but Jacob was eaten up inside with the ugly knowledge he possessed.

This was all Ruth's fault, wasn't it?

It had taken time to piece it all together, but over a year ago, he'd done it.

Betty's funeral had been only a month in the rearview mirror at the time. He wasn't even supposed to be at work the day Suzanne Trifiro had called Harmeling Tree Services. Jacob had been scheduled to take off on a three-day weekend trip with Andy to celebrate their anniversary, but she'd come down with a stomach virus the day before, throwing a wrench in their getaway arrangements. Jacob had tried to stay home as helpful nursemaid, but Andy had insisted he go about his normal routine.

When Jacob's boss sent him on a quote assignment to the home of a woman who'd asked for Jacob by name, he'd assumed it was another referral from loyal customer Lorraine Crockett, an elderly widow with an unladylike crush on Jacob. But then he was sitting in his company truck, checking the address on the appointment paperwork to input into his GPS, and he'd recognized it immediately—only one house down from Ruth's "divorce shack", as she called it, the place she'd bought from some friend or other during her divorce from Stan, husband number two.

Sure enough, when his GPS dropped him at his destination, it was right next door to the charming periwinkle rent house he remembered. The place had been newly-renovated when Ruth made the purchase, meant to be a convenient retreat for vacationers who liked to stay close to the capital city action without being right in the thick of it. It had been small and simple for Ruth's extravagant tastes, but until her accounts through Stan were unfrozen, small and simple had been all she could afford. She went on to live in it after her divorce from Gary, too, renting it out to other tenants in the time in-between.

The woman who answered the door at the Trifiro residence had been nowhere near the age of Lorraine Crockett, but she was in the same ballpark as Ruth. When she saw the name embroidered on Jacob's work polo, she smiled.

"Jacob, it's so nice to meet you. You couldn't deny your mother if you tried; you two look so much alike."

Little time passed before Jacob had all the information he needed: Suzanne was new to the area and had been neighbor to Ruth for only a few weeks before Ruth had ended her stay at the rent house, but they had become fast friends (according to Suzanne—based on some of the stories she relayed to Jacob, he knew his mother had mostly fed the poor woman lies). Ruth had spoken occasionally of Jacob and his occupation—surprising him that his mother hadn't lied about that, too—so when Suzanne had decided to have the strange tree in her backyard appraised for removal, she had known right away who to call.

"I appreciate that," replied Jacob, not knowing what else to say; the woman had clearly meant it as a compliment.

"I've never come across a tree like this," Suzanne remarked as she led Jacob into the backyard, neat with close-cropped grass, perky gnome ornaments, well-tamed shrubbery, and white wicker patio furniture. "I'd have no problem keeping it in tact, but Vinnie-Bear—sorry, that's Vincent, my husband," she paused for a self-conscious giggle, "he hates it. Says it clashes with the environment he's creating for us back here."

Jacob moved his hand smoothly over his mouth to cover his smirk. "Well, I can't pretend to know anything about *that*, but I can tell you that what you have here is one heck of a rarity." He stared at the stubby tree with its hulking trunk and pointy leaves; it wasn't exceptionally tall, but it was far too thick around to remove without equipment and expertise, not to mention the ground at its base was alive with gnarled roots digging in and out of the earth like a den of embedded snakes.

"So you've seen this kind before?" Suzanne's eyes were round with awe. "Vinnie and I tried to identify it with a regional tree encyclopedia, but no luck."

"I've never seen one in person, but I'm positive that this is a Reshawl holly. Must have been imported, because it certainly isn't native to these parts." Jacob adjusted his hat as he turned back to Suzanne; the humidity was daunting that day, sweat already dribbling down his neck and back. "Are you sure about having it removed? Was probably a pretty penny to get it in here, and it'll cost you a prettier penny to get it out."

"I really wouldn't mind keeping it, but Vinnie's mind is made up—and when that man decides to do something, it gets done, come hell or high water." Suzanne looked mournfully at the tree. "A Reshawl holly. I've never heard of such a thing."

Jacob shrugged and walked over to the tree, examining it. "Like I said, it's rare. And it belongs in Europe. I'm surprised this one is making it—our climate is way too hot." He stepped around the back of it, running his fingers down a section without bark.

Suzanne let out a sigh. "I'll be sad to see it go. You know, Ruth loved that tree for some reason, I mean *really* loved it. When I told her Vinnie was thinking of having it hauled off, she threw quite the hissy fit." She began fanning herself with one hand, using the other to lift her hair off her neck. Jacob moved over to her again, stopping a couple feet away. "It was the oddest thing, because a few days later, Vinnie caught Ruth at the mailbox and asked her if she wanted to take the tree for herself, and she told him no, to burn it for all she cared, that it was hideous. Acted as if the conversation with me hadn't happened." Suzanne's face suddenly changed, and she placed her fanning hand on Jacob's forearm. "Oh dear, not that I'm speaking ill of your mother, you understand."

Jacob shook his head. "No, it's all right. I know what you mean." He left it at that, shortly thereafter changing the subject.

Suzanne and her husband donated the tree to Harmeling in the end, asking Jacob to find a new home for it. It wasn't until days later, when Jacob and his coworkers were preparing the tree to be shipped to the buyer they'd found, that he'd remembered what Suzanne had said about his mother: *Ruth loved that tree for some reason, I mean* really *loved it.* Then, Ruth being Ruth, she'd pulled a 180: *She told him no, to burn it for all she cared, that it was hideous. Acted as if the conversation with me hadn't happened.*

Jacob had spent many years on the other end of that same strategy—being told one thing at first, then Ruth would change her mind when the other position suited her better, pretending she'd never taken the opposing stance to begin with.

But she only changed positions when it benefitted her... *when it benefitted her....*

So where was the benefit in that Reshawl holly, and why had Ruth changed her mind about it?

It didn't make sense, and for the rest of the week Jacob rolled it around and around in his mind. What was he missing? Where was the angle his mother was playing at? What was so special about a random European tree?

Money. It had to be about money, Jacob surmised, but then why had she refused to take the tree? She could have easily enough done what Harmeling had done, taken the proffered tree off the Trifiros' hands, and then sold it for a nice sum to any interested party. Ruth was a smart woman; if she didn't take that route, there must have been a better one at her disposal.

That was the moment there had been a click in Jacob's head.

The rectangle of missing bark flashed in his mind's eye.

Disposal.

Of course! It made more sense than anything, and as soon as the idea came, Jacob knew he wasn't wrong. The pieces fit together too flawlessly.

Andy sound asleep beside him and none the wiser, he had laid awake all night sorting out the rest, the story Ruth would never tell him but that he could never un-know.

Reshawl hollies were most revered for their medicinal properties, namely their leaves, useful in treating stubborn skin irritations such as eczema and rosacea. The berries were an excellent agent in fighting indigestion.

Far fewer people knew, however, that the bark of the Reshawl holly, if ingested, was toxic to humans—and, if mixed with the right ingredients, it could be made virtually undetectable.

The timing fit, too. Ruth's divorce from Gary, her return to the rental house, her friendship with Suzanne, the flip-flop of her feelings toward the tree, the rapid decline of Jacob's grandmother's health, her seemingly natural death. It was all there, in a neat line like army ants.

Jacob couldn't be certain how she'd administered it, but there was no doubt: Ruth had poisoned Betty, her own mother, to death.

The scheme was brilliant as it was dark. Jacob's chest had tightened with the severity of it.

The inheritance. Ruth was losing too much money in her divorces; she needed her inheritance allotment sooner than her parents could die. She'd obviously decided to help speed things along. He could see it all now, crystal clear as if it were happening right in front of him.

Ruth must have picked bark off the backside of the tree during her friendship with Suzanne, or she could have done it at night, or when the Trifiros weren't home. How she knew about the toxin Jacob could only guess, but then she'd also found a way to make it into the perfect invisible poison.

As for the actual poisoning part, she would have done it slowly, over the course of months, so as not to raise any alarm. When Betty began to exhibit symptoms of illness, it would have been too late to reverse the effects of the damage —even if she'd been taken straight to the world's best doctors, even if they'd known exactly what was wrong with her, nothing would have stopped the inevitable downward spiral.

But Betty wasn't taken to any doctor, not for a long time. By the time her mental state had begun to deteriorate, the symptoms were identical to Alzheimer's—a nasty case of it, but a clear-cut diagnosis. Unmistakable.

Her death was slow but definite. A natural decline, by everyone's definition. Had it pleased Ruth to see her mother fade away into oblivion like that? Had she been the least bit conflicted over what she'd done? Jacob could only assume she'd saved her tears for the performance of a lifetime: the funeral, where she'd deigned to work her mouth into a frown, sniff loudly, and dab at her mascara-painted eyes with a tissue as though it were all she could do to keep herself together.

The only viable reason she must have refrained from killing two birds with one stone would be to divert any suspicion of foul-play; there would have been an autopsy on both Betty and John otherwise. It was much easier to get away with murder without the involvement of an autopsy, or an investigation, even when utilizing Reshawl holly toxin.

And she had gotten away with it. Famously. Jacob was the only one who knew her secret, and it was because of his silence that she wasn't rotting away in a cell at the moment.

Presently, Jacob sighed, massaging his temples, the ache there pushing against the back of his eyes with every heartbeat. A gust of chilled air collided against him, rifling the pages of Betty's journal in his lap like an accordion come to life. He stretched his hand out to still them, and it was then that something on the paper stole his attention—

I'm so glad Ruthie knows such a great deal about natural remedies for my ailments.

Jacob brought the book nearer to his face, eyes widening as he continued on.

If it weren't for Ruthie's time with the Blasdells all those years ago, I'm sure my arthritis would never be as relieved as it's been since Ruthie began administering her homemade treatments for it. She says the Blasdells taught her all kinds of organic countermeasures, and I believe it. Not only has the arthritis improved, but so has my acid reflux, and my constipation.

Jacob winced as his grandmother went on to praise Ruth's "invaluable help", "generosity", and "kind-hearted devotion". Betty found her daughter's increased presence in her life a blessing, and gushed for pages how providence had seen fit to bring her estranged daughter back to her, even if it was so near the end of her days. She treasured their time together, and longed for more.

Jacob found himself grinding his teeth as he read, hard enough that his jaw got sore.

When he came to the part disclosing more details about his mother's time with these "Blasdells", he was quick to learn how Ruth had known enough to create her toxin. The Blasdells were the elderly couple Dirk had told him about, the ones that owned the plant nursery. They'd taken Ruth in after she left home, treating her like a daughter since they had none of their own. They'd taught her everything they knew about plant life, apparently, and even paid for her to start college, where she'd been studying to become—Jacob blanched—an *arborist*.

Looking up from the journal, he stared off into the burn pile in bewildered silence. Had his mother ever mentioned that to him? Even when he began studying for the same field years later?

He was almost certain she had *not*, and now he knew why.

Chewing on this new intelligence, he skipped ahead in the journal again, turning several pages. When they suddenly became blank, he turned to the last page of Betty's old-fashioned scrawl.

Her notes had become shorter and shorter. The last one read:

I regret so many lost years with my children. I wish I had been a better mother to them. I hate that John—my poor Lone Ranger—will stay distant from them after I am gone. I'm afraid he will die alone in this bed, or on the couch as our daughter did. With the TV on, a sad, lukewarm dinner in his lap. I wanted so much more than this for my family.

With that, Jacob closed the journal. He couldn't take any more. The leather book felt suddenly heavy in his hands, and he debated burying it at the bottom of the burn pile where it would become ash and dust.

But his eyes wandered then to the window of his grandmother's sitting room, her beloved 'Lady Lounge', as Uncle Larry called it.

No. He would keep it. There was incriminating evidence against Ruth now, concrete information straight from the victim's own hand. There may come a day when Ruth needed to pay for her crimes.

If he'd ever really use it against his mother was anybody's guess, but destroying it seemed an unforgivable act against Betty, and in this moment, that was simply something he couldn't do. So, no—he resolved to hide it, keep it safe. Just in case.

It was the least he could do.

CHAPTER TWELVE

ANDY ROCKED BACK AND forth on the bed in Patsy's room, brain skipping like audio on a scratched CD. Her body shook as she fought off tears, a handful of photographs between her fingers in one hand, and her phone in the other.

She still couldn't believe this was happening. She had needed an explanation, and she didn't want to wait for it. Dirk was gone to the store, so that had left one other person in the house without bringing Jacob into it—he already had so much he was dealing with right now. She didn't want to add to his burdens.

Locating Uncle Larry downstairs had been the easy part; the harder business was watching his eyes gloss over the images she showed him and then say, startled if not with confidence, "That's Sarah Marie Whistler. She and Dirk dated in high school. Things ended bad between them; he probably ain't seen or heard from her since."

Feverishly, Andy crushed the photos to her bosom as soon as Uncle Larry's back was turned. "Doesn't he have a child that doesn't speak to him?" Ruth had mentioned something, then Jacob had, too, later on. And there had been that other comment...what was it? She racked her brain, searching for it in her memories of the long day.

Then she remembered: *Even before Patsy died, I was hitched with a bun in the oven—and I didn't even do it out of order.* Larry had responded, *Dirk ain't here yet....*

With a pang in her abdomen, Andy urged herself into the nearest chair.

"Dirk never married," said Uncle Larry. "Though, Sarah Marie...she did have his baby. But her family, they were real high-horse people; moved her off while she was pregnant."

"They did? Why? Why would anyone do that?"

"Didn't wanna face the music around here where everybody knew the truth: their perfect little girl got knocked up by her boyfriend. It's a long story, but the key point is Dirk never met the kid, and Sarah Marie Whistler stayed away all these years."

"Does Dirk know anything about the child?" Fire was blazing along Andy's throat; she clutched the photos so hard they were wrinkling.

"If so, he never shared it with me."

"Not even if it was a boy...or a girl?"

Uncle Larry lifted one shoulder. "Sorry. Dirk put our family in a tight spot with that whole episode. He don't like to bring it up."

"So he...he didn't attempt to find them?" Rage and devastation had a tug-o-war in Andy's chest cavity. Her face was surely white as paper, and she was glad Larry was occupied moving an old upright piano.

"Again, don't rightly know," he said with a grunt.

Dirk was still away, so Andy had tromped back upstairs to Patsy's room where she'd been sorting photos from the box on the bed. That was how she'd discovered the ones of her mother—they were from years ago, from a time Andy had never seen, but she was 99% positive she was not mistaking the chocolate-haired young woman with sparkling blue eyes and a distinctively quirked smile. There had been no identification on the backs of these photos, as there had been with many of the others, so she'd sought out Larry to confirm.

Now she sat on the edge of the mattress unsure of what to do next, feeling like a skeleton that had been picked clean of its flesh. Of all the men and women in the world, her mother...and Jacob's uncle? Andy still couldn't wrap her head around it. She had been raised in another state! She'd never even visited Texas before she moved to Austin for college, and it wasn't as though her mother had pushed her in that direction—it had been a decision Andy had made entirely on her own.

And of all the men I could have met and married in Austin...I chose Dirk's nephew.

Before she could chew any further on the insanity of those odds, the phone in her hand started ringing. She flew off the bed and closed the door to the room, careful to do it quietly, and answered the call.

"Hopefully I'm not interrupting anything too important in Andy Tamblyn's budding, successful life," came the smiling voice of her brother.

"Corey," she breathed. All at once, Andy thought she may fall over. Keeping the emotion in check took every ounce of strength she had; she was forced to clutch the footboard of the bed in order to steady herself. She swallowed with difficulty, her tongue expanding to twice its usual size. "Where are you?"

"Leaving work. Had an early gig today at a retirement party. Excellent tips, though. I tell ya, this Billy Joel starving artist thing may have some crater days, but there are definitely good days, too."

Hearing the chipper cadence of his words, so unaware of

the swaying anvil over their heads, Andy felt like she could break open at any second. She closed her eyes, saying faintly, "That's great, Corey."

"I wanted to tell you, I played my version of that Dave what's-his-name song you sent me, and it was a colossal hit, *colossal!* I'm gonna play that at every gig from now on. Any other recommendations you got for me, I'm all over it."

"Um, sure—I mean, yeah. Whatever you want."

"You sound weird. Something wrong with you?"

What was the point of pretending? Before she could think better of it, she blurted, "I found out something today."

"O-kay? Tell me." He sounded only mildly concerned. She could hear the warbled squall like a dying cat that his jalopy truck made when the door was open, and the scratching sound of movement against the microphone.

"It's kind of a big deal. As in life-changing...."

"Is it?" There was a moment's pause, and then he said in the voice of someone just picking up the punchline of a joke, "Wait—you got that job you were after, didn't you? Didn't you?!"

She realized she must not have spoken to him since she'd been offered the job. "Oh. Well, yes, but—"

"Aww, little Andy got herself a big girl job!" He screeched an outcry of excitement and congratulated her.

"Thanks, Corey, but I really need—"

"Hang on, sorry, my phone is beeping at me. Hold, hooold—dang it, the battery's about to die. I swear, this thing is the bane of my existence. It *never* holds a charge anymore!"

"No, don't let it die. Get hooked up to your charger as soon as—hello? Corey?" She pulled the phone away from her cheek in time to see the call end. Immediately she called back, but was sent straight to voicemail.

"No no no" was her hoarse whisper, pulse beating in her

ears as she dropped the phone onto the bed and held her face in her hands. She began to tremble—not with shock and panic this time, but with anger.

It wasn't Corey she needed to speak to right now anyway, was it?

Heat coursed through her like volcanic lava tubes. With calculated breaths, she retrieved the phone and dialed a different contact. Someone picked up after just a couple rings.

"Hi, baby girl!" Her mother's voice was as upbeat as Corey's had been. "Missing your momma today?"

"Mom."

Sarah didn't catch the stiffness in her daughter's tone. "The whole state of Florida is missing *you*, you know; the weather has been gray and gloomy all week. Must mean you're overdue for a visit!"

"*Mom.*"

Her mother's pause lasted scarcely above a second. "Easy there, grumpster. You must be working too hard at your new job, because it sounds like *somebody* needs a nap...."

"Can you *please*, for just *five minutes of your life*, stop treating me like that four-year-old little girl you used to dress in corduroy overalls and braids with bows at the ends?"

That got Sarah's attention; Andy had heard the stunned suction of her breath through the phone. "Andrea," her mother said, slow and measured, "what's wrong?"

Andy could picture the expression on her mom's face that went with that question. She retreated to the window of Patsy's room as if it would help ground her—though, of course, it didn't. Her vision flitted over the serene neighborhood that had so unexpectedly become hers, and her legs quaked beneath her.

What else about her life was a lie?

That was the question she couldn't shake.

"Andy? Talk to me. Please."

"Momma." Her voice was barely above a whisper, but she didn't trust herself not to cry if she spoke any louder. "Remember when I was seven, and Corey told me we had different parents? He got in trouble, and you swore he was just teasing me, but...I've never forgotten that. Corey didn't seem like he was kidding—I *know* what it's like when he's kidding."

The other end of the line was deathly silent. Andy grit her teeth, summoning strength she didn't know she had as she pressed on.

"Corey and I don't favor much. And he doesn't really favor you. He favors Daddy. And I *don't*...I just look like *you*."

Sarah broke in. "Andy, I think you have the wrong—"

"Mom, please, let me finish. Jacob has an Uncle Dirk. He...there are pictures of you here, in Jacob's grandparents' house. Pictures of *you*...with Dirk."

Sarah let out a tiny gasp, but Andy didn't let it stop her.

"There are pictures of him as kid, too, and they look like...they look like *me*. And Dirk had a child, one he never met. With...*Sarah Marie Whistler*, Mom." Andy's jaw locked up, her face contorting with unshed tears.

"Baby, I can explain." Sarah's words were strained, and smaller than Andy had ever heard out of her mother.

"Just tell me if it's true, please! My *marriage*, Mom...."

"*Andrea*. Calm down. You are *not* Dirk's child."

Andy's lips tightened, and she gripped the phone so hard her knuckles began to pop—but then her brain registered what her mother had said, and it wasn't what Andy had prepared herself for. "Wait, *what?*"

The answering silence throbbed in her ears as though her mother had been screaming into the phone. But when Sarah finally spoke in a hush, her words confirmed the hope Andy had not dared indulge. "Andrea, you are my daughter. You are Stephen Jeffries' daughter. You are not related to Jacob Tamblyn by anything other than marriage."

Andy nearly dropped the phone, such relief flooding through her that she was dizzy. *Oh, thank God! Thank God*. And yet....

"But...these pictures of you and Dirk...and then Larry, he *told* me you had Dirk's baby!"

Her mother took a long, deep, rattling sigh that spoke volumes. "I did, Andy. But the baby wasn't you...."

Then Andy understood. She leaned against the wall by Patsy's window, her free hand going to her forehead in disbelief. "Oh, *Mom*. Does he know?"

"Corey knows. He's always known. Why do you think he told you that when you were seven?"

"Oh my gosh! I just assumed he was saying *I* was the oddball one—I didn't suspect it was *him!*"

The irony of it all was striking. But what relief Andy felt was short-lived, replaced by an acute sense of betrayal most bitter. It was as if someone had stuck a hose in Andy's mouth and filled her full of ice water as she slid her back across the wall, resting against the cool window pane. With her body pressed against it, she felt one with the glass.

"Why did I not know?" She felt her world crumbling to pieces around her, and she was utterly helpless but to stand there and shiver like a child. *Lies, lies, lies!*

"Andy, you have to understand." Sarah sounded desperate, her tone laced with fear. "I was young, still a kid when I met Dirk. Then we fell in love, and...mistakes were made. I got pregnant." She gulped, horrified at her own admission.

"Tell me. The truth."

Sarah took a shuddering breath, and Andy saw in her

mind's eye her mother pacing, hand at her widow's peak, clutching her still-chocolatey hair. "It was a big ordeal. My parents were beside themselves, and *a lot* of drama transpired. Your grandfather decided to move me far away to start over in a new place. He took the family to Arizona, a town where everyone stayed out of everyone else's business. It was perfect for the situation, according to Dad. I tried to fight them on keeping me away from Dirk; I even ran away twice, but they found me. I tried to call him a few times, too, in secret, but each time I left a message with Dirk's brother, and I don't think he gave them to him. I always got the impression he was jealous, that he had a crush on me and resented Dirk for our relationship."

Andy saw a flash of Uncle Larry, wiping sweat from his brow, hauling box after box onto the porch, his stretched t-shirt exposing his plumbers' crack when he bent over to set them down. She heard Ruth's snarling voice say to him in that lofty tone, *What do you got? A shiny bald spot, squinty eyes, and a gut that'd make a pot-belly pig green with envy, that's what!*

She sat on the wide windowsill, her back to the sprawling scene of brown-roofed houses and blacktop roads, dormant, papery lawns, concrete sidewalks bleached by the sun.

Thinking Larry responsible for intentionally choosing not to give Dirk those messages was almost more than Andy's brain could handle at the moment. How could she reconcile the Larry she knew to the Larry her mother spoke of, one who would stoop low enough to play such a game of avarice with other people's lives? But then again, how well did she really know him?

How well did anyone know anyone?

"You really think Larry would do that?" she asked her mother.

Sarah didn't sound pleased to give her answer. "Unfortunately, I do. Why he'd been at the house in the first place to answer those calls was a mystery, because he couldn't have been living there at the time; but that's neither here nor there."

Andy didn't *want* to believe it, but somehow, maybe instinctually, she knew he'd done it—deliberately withheld life-altering information from his own brother, getting in the way of what could have been an opportunity for Dirk and Sarah to reunite had Larry acted with honor.

It made Andy feel double-crossed and untrusting of the man, and slightly more sympathy for Sarah. "What happened next, Mom?"

"I wrote Dirk a letter, and it came back. My parents were furious with me, so I didn't try that again, just in case. But when I didn't hear from Dirk, I began losing hope. It took a few weeks, but I realized I wasn't one of those independent young women that could raise a baby on my own, and if Dirk wouldn't or couldn't help me, then what could I do but stay?" Sarah's voice took on an astringent tone. "My parents convinced me it was the right thing to do to write Dirk a different letter, to officially end things. I told him that neither I, nor the baby, would have contact with him. For all I knew, it was what he wanted, because I didn't hear a word from him."

Andy realized she was chewing one of her fingernails to the quick on her free hand, so she dropped it to the windowsill and moved to pin it down with her thighs.

"I had Corey my senior year of high school, and graduated through a homeschool program with a private tutor Dad hired. I accepted my family's help until they started interfering too much with how I wanted to raise my son. I took that as my cue to strike out on my own, so when Corey was a year old, I found a small women's college in Michigan that was ideal for young, single mothers."

"Mom...how did you make it?" Andy was breathless

listening to her mother's story, the one she'd never suspected, much less heard. With every word, she felt her anger ebbing away, like Sarah was chipping at it with a chisel.

"Well," said Sarah, "I'd been saving every nickel I could get my hands on since I'd found out I was pregnant, knowing that one day I'd need to get away for good. So I packed what I could fit into one suitcase, took Corey, and off we went to Michigan. I got a roommate who was also a single mom, and she was older, so she made a great mentor for me. She taught me how to manage money, my time, and balance my schedule with being a student and a working mom. I worked full-time in the mornings at a travel agency around the corner from my apartment, did all my undergrad via night classes, studied really hard, then I earned a full-ride scholarship for grad school in Alabama—that's where I ran into one of my old classmates from high school.

"It was the first I'd heard anything about Dirk since before I'd written the letter. My friend told me he spent all his money the summer after high school searching for me, but that he came back empty-handed. From what she knew, he'd given up after that, started a job locally in some factory, lived there, and was still single and sad. After that, I couldn't stop thinking about him. I'd been able to keep him off my mind the last few years with how busy I was, but underneath it all, I still wasn't over the guy. I felt pathetic, and it made me a little nuts for awhile trying to bury all the old memories. I poured myself into my grad work and Corey, and when that still wasn't enough, I took up working two part-time jobs to keep my mind *really* occupied. I was still working in the travel industry for one job, and the other was nights waiting tables at a diner on the weekends. I...I met your dad on that job."

"You did?" It was hard to imagine—Andy's parents,

younger than her, at a mom and pop restaurant in Alabama, making eyes at each other over milkshakes and French fries. "I thought you guys met in college?"

"*In* college, yes. Not *at* college." A smile crept into Sarah's voice. "He was so charming, and boy, was he patient with me. He came in every Friday, Saturday, and Sunday night to sit in my section and ask me out, even knowing I'd say no."

"You said *no?*"

"I was in no condition to date, believe me, Andy. I was a wreck. I'd kept men at bay since I'd moved away from Texas, and I had no intention of changing that. But," she said, suddenly wistful, "it was Stephen Jeffries that got me thinking about what I really wanted out of my love life. I contemplated it for weeks...and I kept coming back to Dirk."

Andy's heart lurched. "You contacted him," she guessed out loud.

"He was my son's father. And now that I knew what he'd done, that he *hadn't* just cut me and Corey loose after all, that he'd tried to find us...I had to know, had to see if maybe...we could..." She took a deep breath and cleared her throat. "Anyway. I wrote him another letter. I had to send it to his parents' house because I didn't know how else to reach him, but this time—in case anyone was out to sabotage me still—I tucked it inside a secondary envelope that was addressed to his mom, since she always liked me a lot, and included a note requesting she get it to him as soon as possible."

Sarah faltered then, and several moments passed before she went on haltingly, "I don't know what went wrong next. Maybe she didn't honor my wishes and threw the letter away, or could be that she did forward it to him, and *he* threw it away. Maybe he read it first, maybe he didn't. Or he could've kept it, but he didn't read it—perhaps it was years later when he finally had the backbone to open it up and see what I had to say, or he could still have it somewhere, sitting in a drawer unopened. I just don't know. What I *do* know…is that I asked him to meet me in Mississippi. I asked him to meet his son for the first time. I gave him the address, the date, the time, everything. Corey and I drove hours and hours to get there; I didn't tell Corey why, of course, though he did ask me. It's a good thing he didn't know, because…because Dirk never showed." Her voice cracked, the sound squeezing Andy's lungs. "He *didn't come*."

Tumultuous emotions Andy didn't even have names for burned through her veins like acid. "*Oh*, Momma…."

"I didn't try again to reach out to him," said Sarah, now resigned. "I was extra glad I'd been cautious and hadn't told him where Corey and I really were, because after he didn't show up…I never wanted to see him or hear from him again. I was so heartbroken—but it was what I needed to move forward. It was the closure I'd been holding out for since I was seventeen. And…and it pushed me toward your father. When Corey and I got back to Alabama, the next time Stephen Jeffries asked me on a date, I sat down at his table, pulled his face towards me, and kissed him.

"I didn't let him call me Sarah Marie; I insisted on Sarah. Stephen met Corey after a couple months, and they fell in love with each other. I'd lost touch with my family by then, which seemed to work fine for both parties, so I didn't even tell them when Stephen and I got married. I didn't tell them when we moved to Florida after I finished grad school, either. I wanted everything about my past besides Corey to stay right where it belonged—behind me. I became Sarah Jeffries and never looked back. I had you, and…I didn't want you to know about any of it."

Sarah took a shuddering breath. "It was simpler that way, for all of us. I convinced your dad, and we told Corey it would be our little secret, the three of us, that Stephen wasn't his birth father. When you asked us questions we couldn't answer without giving something away, we gave you vague answers and deflections." A hollow pain entered her voice. "We always knew there was a chance that one day you'd find out, but...you just kept getting older and older, and I started to think maybe...."

"Maybe I'd never have to know."

"Oh, Andy." Sarah released another dragging exhale that rustled the microphone. "I'm so sorry, baby girl. Truly. I still don't know if it was wrong or right of me to keep it from you, but I am sorry that *my* secrets have caused *you* pain." She broke down then, the sounds of her tears echoing through the receiver and rattling around in Andy's skull as if nothing else existed.

She stood, the low sun pelting her back, outlining her shape on the dusty wooden floor within the bright square of the window. Her eyes drifted upward as though called, settling on the mattress where she'd left the old photographs. She floated across the floorboards towards them, her fingers reaching out of their own accord to touch one of Sarah and Dirk, the two of them wrapped up in each other's arms, their cheeks pressed tightly together, their laughing grins larger than life.

"Jacob doesn't know. I don't think Dirk knows, either."

She gave Sarah time to collect herself. "I can hardly believe it myself," Sarah sniffed at last. "Jacob Tamblyn is Dirk's nephew. All this time you've been together, and I had no idea. It seems so impossible! Of all the people in the world...."

"...We still found each other," Andy finished for her.

"And Corey is Jacob's cousin. First cousin!"

Andy shivered. "Don't remind me. I was afraid that *I* was his cousin at first, you know."

Sarah gave a tired laugh, but then she asked breathlessly, "Are you planning to tell them?"

Andy's eyes were still glued to Dirk's face in the photo at her fingertips. His honesty from earlier reverberated through her: *So many things I'd do different.*

"What do *you* want me to do, Mom?"

"He didn't come, Andy" was all her mother would say.

CHAPTER THIRTEEN

JACOB KNEW WHO HAD lived in the last bedroom the moment the door swung open with a whine. Both his uncles had been avoiding this room all day, helping him with his guesswork. Their aversion was his gain, though, as it was the last place for Jacob to search. His sweep of the room would need to be fast before anyone got the idea to join him. *This has to be it. If they aren't here, he threw them away.*

His head was beginning to pound, the day's events proving to be far more than his overworked mind could cope with. It didn't help knowing that the more time that passed, the greater the chances that someone else would stumble across what he was looking for. And if they were *touched*....

To think of being responsible for even a day of madness for one more person sent shivers down Jacob's spine.

He'd been careful, keeping himself as focused and calm as possible—well, with the exception of the blowout with Ruth. But that had always been unavoidable from the start, something he'd enfolded into the plan just to be safe. Everything would be easier without Ruth around; if she got wind of what he was up to, what he'd done…there was a possibility, however microscopic, that she would ruin everything.

Worst case scenario, he could kiss his brightening future with Andy goodbye. No more house, no moving up at Harmeling towards becoming an actual arborist, no financial freedom, no kids someday—and worst of all, no more Andy. She'd never speak to him again, wouldn't want to be near him or even look at him, much less visit him in prison. It wouldn't matter to her that he'd done all of this solely for them, for her, to give her something closer to the life she deserved. He wanted that more than anything.

And, as he'd told her, he would do whatever it took to make her happy.

Trying to limit the noise he made so as not to draw extra attention from the others, Jacob inched his way around the room, checking in all the obvious places—drawers, cabinets, the closet. As expected, the room was bursting with boxes and junk, if not less overwhelming than the rest of the house. The time it took to go through the stacked boxes, to move things around and check the nooks and crannies, didn't take as long as he'd feared, but it didn't matter either way—the search turned up nothing.

He muttered a curse under his breath, throwing the lid of the last box across the room. It landed on a pile of folded quilts in one corner with a muted *thud*. Without thinking better of it, he flung himself down on the bed, exhausted as he was discouraged. Minimal dust went flying, another indication of Jacob's Granddaddy living in here when he died. It set his nose to itching and reached down into his throat, making him cough. He was compelled to sit up—and his legs collided with something sharp poking out just so from between the mattress and the box spring.

Scowling as the coughing subsided, he rubbed the tender

spot on his calf with one hand, and used the other to feel around the side of the bed for the protruding object. When his fingers caught the edge of something like the corner of a book, he bent over and lifted the blanket that shielded it. His heart stopped.

Finally, he'd found them.

The letters.

Jacob could have cried, or broken out in song and dance—both felt appropriate at the moment. He was thankful he hadn't yet removed his gloves in his aggravation as he slid off the bed and gently pried the letters out. They were all together, as he'd suspected they might be, tied into a little stack with brown string. He untied the string and counted them out—indeed, all were present and accounted for. He also checked that inside the envelopes was every page of every letter—yes, good.

There was a box nearby with newspaper sticking out of it; Jacob pulled out first one sheet, folded it in half, tucked the letters inside, and then made a ball around them with three more sheets. The stale aroma of the old paper and ink permeated his nostrils as he worked.

When he stuck his head out of the bedroom minutes later, the hallway was still and no one was around; he could hear Uncle Larry still thumping about downstairs, his thundering footsteps not unlike a badly-choreographed Goliath tap routine in the quiet house. Holding the ball of disguised letters, Jacob approached Patsy's room at the front of the hall. He was relieved to see the door closed, and hear a soft, garbled voice on the other side; Andy must be on the phone with someone from her new office. The timing couldn't have been more perfect.

He slunk past the door and down the stairs, coming up on Uncle Larry in the living room.

The older man jabbed his chin toward the ball Jacob held

as if it were a bomb and inquired curiously, "Whatcha got there?"

"Another furry houseguest—still alive, I think, but unconscious. We had a tiff upstairs."

Exactly as Jacob had hoped, Uncle Larry staggered backward and let out a frazzled gasp, his eyes huge as they snapped to the newspaper ball.

"Don't worry, Uncle Larry, I thought I'd take him to the burn pile out back. We've got other stuff we could burn; may as well get the thing going while it's still daylight."

"Good—good idea."

Keeping up the charade, Jacob took careful, quick steps all the way to the backyard and up to the burn pile. It was smaller than what they probably needed for all the paper junk they'd gone through in the house, but there was plenty to get started—and more than enough to burn a handful of poisoned letters.

CHAPTER FOURTEEN

ANDY WASN'T SURE OF the last time her heart had felt so exhausted. It was as though she'd run a marathon with a sumo wrestler on her back; even breathing hurt.

She was still holed up in Patsy's room, trying to sort through the constellation of her thoughts and rest her fried emotions. There were still countless things to do in this room, but she felt her ambition waning. The temptation to lay across the dusty, photo-cluttered bedspread of Patsy's bed and go to sleep was almost too inviting to pass up.

But she refrained. Instead, she steered clear of the bed altogether, and sifted through what remained of Patsy's jewelry. Patsy's taste was so different than anything Andy had seen on Ruth, and she couldn't imagine any of the pieces being donned by her mother-in-law, at this or any age.

"Knock, knock," said a voice.

Uncle Larry poked his head into the room and gave her a little wave. "Hey, got any more trash bags hiding up here? Dirk still ain't back from the store."

Upon seeing his face, animosity roared to life in Andy's naval. She had felt it earlier after hearing of his old deceptions from her mother, but now it was back in full force. Her expression hardened, and Larry blinked in surprise.

"Everything okay?"

All sense demanded Andy let it go, that she keep her mouth shut, give him her last trash bag, and send him on his way without confrontation.

But that wasn't what happened.

"Did you have feelings for Sarah Marie Whistler?"

Uncle Larry's face went slack. "Pardon?"

"I said, did you have feelings for Sarah Marie Whistler?"

"I—Well, I don't—Why would you ask that?" He sputtered, his small eyes rounding enough that they almost appeared to be a normal size.

"I have reason to believe you did," Andy replied in a clipped voice. "That she reached out to your brother after her family carted her away, and you interfered. So I'm asking, did you have feelings for her? Because I can't think of any other reason why someone would do such a shameful thing."

Jacob's uncle wrung his hands, eyes darting about the room like a cornered animal searching for an escape route. "Well, I just—I—I don't wanna talk about this."

"You did it, didn't you? You deliberately kept Sarah's messages from Dirk!"

"But I didn't!"

"Yes, you did! I know you did! Your face says it all."

Larry swallowed, and his face fell into a deep frown, his jowls shivering. "How'd you know?"

An admission. Andy had expected to feel some relief, but she only felt the sharp bite of despair. "Does it matter? Larry, how could you? How could you have kept them apart like that? You knew they loved each other!"

"They was seventeen, eighteen-years-old. Kids! Dirk didn't know nothing about raising a baby. He was better off."

He didn't believe his own words, but she could tell he wanted to. He wanted them to be true so badly.

She wanted to shake him. "That's not why you did it. Tell the truth."

"That is the truth!"

"*Stop lying!*" The shout rang through the room, echoing into the halfway, bouncing off the living room walls and filling the belly of the house like poison gas. Andy shook her head from side to side, hearing how out of control she sounded. She took a calming breath and said more steadily, "You're caught, Larry. Just admit it. You liked her, too."

Pain flashed a poignant streak across Larry's features. "No, I didn't, I loved her, that's what! I loved her first!"

"First?" The news pushed Andy backward, her feet tripping over themselves as if she'd been shoved by a pair of invisible hands.

"Yes, all right? I met her first. I introduced her to Dirk. Lord, I wish I hadn't." He closed his eyes, the agony in his expression so ripe it was as though the whole thing had happened yesterday. Somehow, it was still fresh, even after all this time.

"I don't get it. How did you even get involved? You weren't living at home anymore by that time."

"No," agreed Larry, "but I had stopped by Ma and Pop's one day to pick up some mail they had for me. Sarah Marie called while I was here, and I answered."

"So you lied to her? Pretended you'd give Dirk her messages, although you knew you wouldn't?" It was impossible to keep the judgment from her tone.

Larry scowled and looked toward the window, hands on his broad hips. "I didn't plan not to tell him at first, thank you very much. But then Sarah Marie told me when she'd call again to talk to Dirk, that she could only get away certain days at certain times. Once I knew that, I...just wanted to

123

hear her voice again. So I made sure I was at the house the next time she called."

"And what did you tell her when Dirk wasn't there to speak to her like she asked?"

"I told her I'd asked him to come, but that he'd refused. She told me to beg him. The next time she called, I told her the same thing, that he still didn't wanna talk. After that, she just hung up, and she didn't call again. I came back to Ma and Pop's every Thursday at 4:00 for weeks afterward, but no more calls came."

Andy's jaw clenched. "And the letter she sent?"

Larry wouldn't meet Andy's eyes. "I marked it return to sender."

Nails cutting into her palms like minuscule razor blades, Andy turned away from him and sat on the edge of the bed with her back to him. "You could have found someone else. There were other girls, Larry."

His tone was hollow as he responded, "Not like Sarah Marie."

The confession tore at Andy's heart with an unapologetic ferocity that made her eyes water. She knew the splendor that was her mother. She knew of her beauty, her irresistible charm, the tinkling bell-like quality of her laugh, the radiance of her smile. The enchantment of it all had been cast over Larry, and to him it had never worn off. "Is that why you never married?"

"Why do you care anyway?" The words flew at her like daggers, and when she turned around to look at him, she recognized the sting of humiliation etched into the purse of his lips, the crinkle of his nose, the furrow in his brow. "This is none of your business—you weren't even alive yet."

"Maybe not," she said with a toss of her head, "but I do care. Dirk's son is out there, and it's because of you that he doesn't know him."

At that, Larry froze, absorbing the information and trying to come up with his own explanation for it. "How do you know it was a son?"

Andy contemplated telling him, just coming out with the full story right then and there. But she heard her mother's pleading voice over her recklessness, and she bit her tongue. "I—I just know, all right? He's also your nephew, Larry. Don't you want to know him yourself? Just a little?"

Larry's face contorted, his skin colored in deep hues of purple and red. He collapsed into the rocking chair by the bed, which creaked angrily like a goose in a headlock, sounding as though it may shatter into splinters at any moment. "Of course I do."

Andy rose and took a small step toward him. "Maybe it's not too late?"

His face was a picture of utter hopelessness as he said, "But it is. It was too late the second after I did it. They'd never forgive me, Andy."

"How can you be sure of that?" Even as she said it, she guessed Larry was right—they wouldn't forgive him. Not for a long time, if ever.

"We wasn't taught much about forgiveness, you know, growing up. Swerving around the hard stuff, that's what we was taught. And it was so long ago, anyhow. Dirk's made his peace with it. I'd be a mighty bad brother to do that to him now, shake up his life like that."

Although she knew there was a certain amount of truth to that, it irked Andy that Larry was so quick to give himself an out. "None of this would have happened if you had just let them be at the start!" she snapped. "You lost. Sarah Marie made her choice. Why couldn't you just move on?"

Larry surged out of the rocking chair, towering over her at his tallest height. "Look here, missy. You may think you know it all, that you got the whole thing figured out, but the heart wants what it wants. You try telling a twenty-some-thing guy to find another woman sometime. See how that works out for you!"

"Life is hard, Larry! We all make sacrifices."

"Yeah, well, screw that!"

"She didn't love you! She loved—"

"What's going on in here?"

Both of them spun toward the direction of the voice, rattled by being caught in such a heated moment.

Eyes wide with a mixture of alarm and curiosity, Dirk filled the doorway, glancing back and forth between his brother and Andy.

"I'm outta here." Before another word could be spoken, Larry bolted from the room at a speed quite admirable in consideration of his size.

"What on earth was that about? Or dare I ask?"

Andy scrutinized Dirk's face, determining whether or not he'd overheard too much of the argument. She guessed he hadn't heard anything important, or else his expression would be quite different.

"It's nothing." She crossed her arms, feeling as if she'd split in half right down the middle of her body if she didn't.

"Well, I hope 'nothing' gets resolved by tomorrow. Or else I'm coming back here with ear plugs."

The letters had burned first, the kindling that caught the entire burn pile and set it ablaze.

Jacob was an expert at managing brush fires thanks to his occupation, so it was crackling merrily with flames past his shoulders when Uncle Dirk appeared beside him.

Daylight was fading out into a strawberry and orange dreamsicle sunset, and the crisp autumn air was getting cooler by the minute. Leaves stirred at their feet, dancing in the twirling skirts of a free-spirited wind.

"Larry and your wife got into it, FYI."

Jacob turned to Dirk sharply. "What?"

Uncle Dirk nodded, amused. "Don't know what got them started, or what the spat was even about, but they was sure invested. Walked in on them yelling in each other's faces when I came back from the store."

"That's...unexpected," said Jacob, completely taken aback. Andy was so civil, the first to try for peace in most situations. "I should go in and talk to her—"

"Aw, leave it. She'll be all right, kiddo. Sheesh." Dirk snickered good-naturedly. "I know she's your wife and all, but she can get by without you occasionally. She's a strong lady. Let her be strong."

Jacob stared at Dirk for a long moment before returning his gaze to the fire. He fed more trash to the blaze with careful movements, both men stepping back when the flames spit large embers back at them like a feral cat.

"What do you know about the Blasdells?" Jacob asked suddenly, switching gears instinctually to his grandmother's journal. There was an opportunity here with Dirk that Jacob didn't want to pass up.

"Well," Uncle Dirk began, "can't say I know much, but they're the ones I was telling you about that took Ruthie under their wings for a spell."

"They owned a plant nursery, right?"

"They did, yes."

"How did she know them, anyway?"

Dirk scratched his chin. "Let's see. I believe she interviewed to rent a property of theirs. The little house right next door to where her 'Divorce Shack' is. You know it?"

The Trifiros' house?

Oh. That explained a lot.

127

"Yes. I know it."

"They lived next door, in the house she owns now, and they rented out the one beside it. Then they remodeled theirs, and sold it to Ruthie. Dunno if they still rent out the other."

"No...I've met the couple that lives there now. They own the place."

"Oh. Well, you know about as much as me, then."

"Did you know my mom went to school to be an arborist?"

Dirk's brows jerked upward. "Shoot. No, I didn't know that. Did she encourage you to go to school for that?"

"That's what I keep trying to remember. But no, I really don't think she did. She didn't even keep plants when I was growing up. It's weird."

Dirk slapped Jacob's arm and let out a warm laugh. "Son, if that momma of yours made sense half as much as she was supposed to...."

Jacob's lip lifted. "Yeah."

CHAPTER FIFTEEN

THE SKY WAS ALIGHT with pink and gold streaks, sun barely visible over the treetops in the distance when Andy dragged herself away from the window. She'd been watching it set for some time, but she hadn't seen it happen.

On autopilot, she began to collect the photos from the bed to return them to their box; only a few remained atop the faded bedspread when there was a knock at the bedroom door.

"It's open." Her voice sounded thin and strained even to her own ears, so when Jacob sailed in, she wasn't surprised by the concern in his eyes. "I'm fine," she said before he could ask, and replaced the last of the photos in the box. The lid slid into place just as Jacob drew up behind her, his breath warm on her neck.

Her deflection was wasted effort on him. "No, you're not 'fine'." He spun her around, arms already encircling her shoulders, and analyzed her face. She thought she saw a flicker of angst cross his features as he spared a glance down at the box, but it was gone as quickly as it had appeared.

Surely he didn't know about her mother and Dirk, about Corey...

...Or could he?

"Come on, it's me," he prodded with a kiss to her temple. "What's up with you?"

Andy swallowed, her insides frozen by uncertainty. "I don't know...."

Jacob's eyes bore into her like a physical force she could feel in her chest.

She cleared her throat. "Today has been kinda crazy. I guess everything is culminating." She dropped her gaze, an unpleasant heaviness settling on her with that partial truth.

Jacob tilted his head, and she couldn't be positive, but it seemed he was indirectly looking at the box again. She cut her eyes to catch him—but he was staring placidly at her, waiting. She wriggled out of his arms with a delicate grace he wouldn't take offense to; she suddenly found herself needing space, Jacob's proximity an inhibitor for clear thought at the moment.

"I can understand that," her husband said. He followed her with his eyes as she zig-zagged around the room finding unwanted odds and ends suitable for a future rummage sale. "Too much to process for a Saturday, huh?"

"Yeah, I guess." She paused. "And I just don't get it, babe—why would your grandfather care that we all participated in cleaning out this house? What's so satisfying about bringing a bunch of people that mostly despise each other under one roof just to make nice so they can legally check off a box? Why would he care about something like that after he's dead?"

Jacob brewed over the question before saying at last, "Maybe it wasn't for him. Maybe he wanted to give his wife something he didn't give her in life—a family that struggled together as a team instead of as individuals."

Andy's mouth fell open. "That seems...oddly specific."

Shrugging, Jacob said blandly, "I could be wrong. If I had all the answers, we would've been rich a long time ago." He took a step toward the bed, examining the lidded box of photos.

Andy's limbs seized up.

"What's in here? Is it really photos? The box says photos." His tone was conversational, inquisitive—but his hand rested on the lid, poised to open it.

Andy schooled her expression into nonchalance, choosing her next words carefully as she scooted over to him in one smooth stride and twisted his free arm around her waist in a relaxed hug. "Photos of strangers from the 80s. Clippings from magazines and newspapers, stuff like that. I think someone was planning to make an extravagant collage or something, maybe a pop culture scrapbook? Anyway, boring. I was thinking of sending it down to the Scrapper Ladies' Club. I bet they could use it."

"Sure. I'll take it for you on Monday."

"No!" Andy had to work fast to reign in her alarm; she smiled with a light laugh for good measure. "Thanks for the thought, but I'd better do it myself. You will have enough on your plate around here without me sending you on more errands."

"I doubt I'll mind," Jacob said. His other hand still rested on the lid of the box; Andy's heart beat so hard she could feel it in her ears.

"I'll have a list a mile long of honey-dos for you over the next few days; trust me, you won't have the time. Besides, I should go through the box one more time to make sure I didn't miss anything of value."

"I could do that for you right now?" Jacob's suggestion was accompanied by a move to take off the box's lid, and

Andy's belly panged like she was going downhill on a roller coaster.

"Really, babe, we have bigger fish to fry." She kissed the side of his mouth tenderly, hoping to God it would distract him. "And you *know* how I am about pictures. Better not get in my way, or you'll wake that sleeping beast, the testy control freak you love so much."

Jacob laughed, if not somewhat strained, and planted a solid kiss on her mouth. "As you wish, highness."

He removed his hand from the box, unwound himself from Andy, and sat down in the rocking chair.

Andy could have burst into tears of gratitude, but wisely kept her expression committed. "So...where are your uncles?"

"I sent them home. We moved all the trash boxes from the porch to the street, and it's almost dark. They've worked hard enough for one day. They aren't as young and sprightly as I am."

"Oh." Andy couldn't tell if the rush of blood to her head was because of consolation or regret.

Jacob quirked his brow, and she wondered if he knew what had transpired between her and Larry. "I think they were ready to get out of here. Long day for all of us."

"They'll be back tomorrow?"

"Sure." Jacob scratched at his chin, his five o'clock shadow growing in. "Larry seemed a little out of sorts. I think today really tuckered him out. And Dirk was a bit more pensive than usual."

Andy took a deep breath. She opened her mouth to tell him about Larry, but then she had another thought. "Dirk and I had a long talk today. About...your family."

Jacob blinked. "Oh?"

Andy shrugged, again playing up the nonchalance. "He told me a little about his childhood here, his relationship with the siblings. Even shared with me about Patsy."

"Patsy?"

"Your aunt. She was the oldest of the siblings—you never met her."

"I know who she was."

Andy's throat went desert dry. "Um, right. Well. Since this was her room, it got us talking."

"About Patsy?"

"Among other things…but her story really struck me. It was just so devastating, you know? Her life was lonely and isolated. And then Dirk, he said no man wanted her, not in her whole life. She never married, never had kids, maybe never fell in love…just worked a desk job and ate TV dinners alone in her apartment." Andy chewed her lip. "She *died* like that, Jacob—just a regular day, doing what she always did. Watching TV, and boom! Brain aneurysm. How unfair is that?"

As soon as the words came out, Andy realized how true every bit of it was. It was more than an excuse to feed her husband—she needed to get these things off her chest.

"Then I kept thinking about your grandmother, that journal, how she must have just wanted not to be vacant at the end, how she was trying not to lose herself, but it happened anyway. And then your grandfather? The end of his life wasn't so different." She pressed a hand to her sticky forehead, pacing, reminding herself of her mother. "Being up close and personal in their house like this, where they raised kids and lived this crazy-simple lifestyle for decades—it makes me confused, like I'm simultaneously violating and preserving what's left of so many past lives here. It's thrown me into this whirlwind of emotion, and I…it's just…was it all meaningless?" She gestured to the mauve walls and the iron bed, the rose-shaped rug under her feet. "Is this all we amount to when we're gone? Dust-covered rooms that people come behind us and tear apart as if nothing in it ever mattered, just because it doesn't matter to *them*...it's unbearable."

She saw the way Jacob's lips were pursed, his lids half-closed as he fought to make sense of her ramblings. His face was a solid mask of concentration.

Andy rubbed her eyes and exhaled.

"Maybe this is what an existential crisis is like, I don't know. But I'm smothered—by my own thoughts, my feelings. It's like I've been suspended in outer space, and I looked down on Earth and all I saw was the frailty of life, the complexity of humanity, the penalties of hindsight, and...I'm just trying to make the right decisions. Right now it all feels like more than I can handle."

Moments passed without a word from Jacob. The wind outside picked up, rattling the window pane. Andy tugged her fingers past her temples, through her tangled mess of hair, matted with sweat, dust, and grime. She'd never longed so passionately for a shower.

Jacob rose from the rocking chair, his countenance one of understanding as he ushered Andy into his arms for what could have been the hundredth time in a day as easily as the fifth. With a harrowed sigh, Andy leaned into the familiar comfort, one thing in life she could always count on.

"So...is that why you and Uncle Larry got into a verbal sparring match?"

Ugh. The scent of sweat and campfire smoke filled her senses as she muttered in embarrassment, "Pretty much."

"Sorry it's been a tough day, babe."

"It is what it is. No use crying over spilled milk, is there?"

Jacob squeezed her a little tighter. "Is that everything you have to say?"

Andy tensed ever so slightly, and she prayed Jacob didn't notice. "Well...um, I guess...I have one more confession to make."

Her pulse thrummed in her veins so powerfully she could have sworn there was a rushing river flowing inside her body. Jacob leaned back to look at her, and his gaze held her firmly, unblinking.

"I've always resented you for not giving me more details about your family. After today...I think I'm better off not knowing everything."

After a long, thoughtful look at his wife, the skin around Jacob's eyes crinkled up. He chuckled. "You know, they say ignorance is bliss."

Andy dipped her chin downward so he wouldn't see her eyes pooling with tears.

"I'd say there's no better evidence of that than with family. Those we love," he added.

Taking a hard swallow against Jacob's collarbone, Andy responded, "You're probably right."

Strong fingers hooked beneath Andy's chin, forcing her eyes to meet her husband's. Reliably, they were the same stormy gray they'd always been, which soothed her.

"I love you, Andy."

Andy let those words fill her up from top to bottom, absorbing them into the tightest knots of her spirit. "I love you, Jacob."

"No more secrets?"

She wanted to gulp in extra air, but she didn't. "No more secrets."

"I think you should call it a night, too."

"Go home without you?"

"Why not? You've worked as hard as Larry and Dirk; you deserve it. And don't forget, I have dead rodents to clean up downstairs."

"Ew, that's right." Andy grimaced. "Still. There's so much left to do up here."

"It'll be here tomorrow." Jacob pressed a kiss to her lips, tasting of salt. "Go on. I'll take an Uber home."

"You're sure? I mean, I have no problem staying—"

"No way," persisted Jacob. "Get home, take a bubble bath, eat some chocolate, drink hot tea, turn in early. Doctor's orders."

Andy kissed him again, lingering long enough to run her fingers through hair that matched hers in grunginess. "Okay then, Dr. Tamblyn. Off I go." She released him and marched over to the box of photos, hoisting it into her arms with a grunt. She winked at Jacob. "Just in case you get any ideas of helping me against my wishes."

He laughed. "Will you at least let me carry it down the stairs and to the car for you?"

Andy smiled, eyes twinkling, mood already improving. "I suppose I can allow that."

∼

When Andy was safely sent off down the street in the car, Jacob turned back to the house with a renewed sense of purpose. But he had barely stepped one foot through the front door when his phone rang.

He groaned. "What now?"

Much to his chagrin, the screen read the very last name he was expecting to see: RUTH.

His finger hovered over the REJECT button, but just before the call went to voicemail, he hit ANSWER.

"What, Ruth?" was his tactless opening line.

"What a way to talk to your mother," came Ruth's husky drawl, though Jacob thought he detected a hint of a slur.

"Can I help you with something?" he prompted again, hoping she hadn't been drinking. Ruth was a nightmare with alcohol in her.

"Jake," said Ruth, her voice breathy and strange, "do I really get my money? Even though you kicked me out? I'm scared." Her voice quivered, and for the first time all day, Jacob thought it could have been sincere. "That Marsden man said we all have to meet the terms of the will, right? But I didn't, because of you. But I need that money, Jake. I've been through so much...I *need* it."

Jacob leaned against the wall where he stood, his back pressing against several of the decorative crosses. He hardly registered the discomfort. "Ruth, are you drunk right now?"

"I've had a martini, that's all," she replied. "But I'm not drunk."

"You'll get your money, Ruth. I gave you my word."

There was a strangled sound on the line, and then Ruth was laughing; but it wasn't her usual derisive, condescending laugh. It was genuine elation. "Thank you, Jake. You're not half as sorry as your Granddaddy."

The connection went dead in his ear.

CHAPTER SIXTEEN

THE HUSH OF THE old house was hefty now that Jacob was alone. It settled over him like a thick woolen blanket in the peak of summer's heat, stifling, stealing his breath. He'd been standing, nose to wood, in front of the door to Betty's lounge for an infinite moment. His hand was poised over the ring of keys buried inside his pocket, but he couldn't bring himself to take them out, insert the one flecked with yellow paint into the lock.

Jacob's legs felt like wet sandbags. His head was in a vice of two giant hands, the tension pressing, pressing on his brain, sending feverish thoughts circling around him like insatiable ghosts.

Had it really come to this? Would this be the way of his family until no one remained? A clothesline of selfish motives strung up behind each unforgivable act, hidden truths of unspeakable magnitude taken to early graves, each cadaver lowered into the ground with more secrets than the last.

Jacob didn't know who to crown as the worst of them. His own guilt was undeniable as it was inexcusable in the light of day, but his plan would never have been born had it not been for his inadvertent discovery of Ruth's hand in his grandmother's demise.

But he couldn't place the blame on her for his actions.

For the day after Jacob had learned of his mother's part in Betty's illness and subsequent death, he had been distracted from the moment he woke up to the moment he fell asleep, hours after crawling into bed, thoroughly sleep-deprived but overpowered by restlessness. He had found himself broken in half by what he'd learned—one half of him dismayed, shattered by the sheer heartlessness his mother's plot had brought to light; yet the second half of him revealed the unthinkable, the blackest recesses of his heart, something he'd never known he was capable of: a growing hunger, an instinct to capitalize on circumstance, to play the lucky hand he'd found so unpredictably at his fingertips. To change the tide, seize the moment, to drink the potion—

To finish what his mother had started, not for her, but for himself—for his selfless wife, the woman he thought the world of, wanted to give the world *to*.

Andy deserved the best of everything, and Jacob had needed more money than what he had to give it to her. Arborists did well for themselves, but he wasn't certified yet and wouldn't be for awhile. What he'd needed was a jump-start to get them rolling. His part of the family inheritance would be meager compared to his mother and her siblings, but it would be a fine nest egg. His grandmother had told him that more than once, and his grandfather had confirmed it in recent years.

Ruth had been too impatient to wait for it—maybe he was, too, now that another option had presented itself.

It was crazy, awful, cruel, despicable. He'd known it, felt it in every inch of himself. And if he wasn't careful, it could all come crumbling down as quickly as it had taken shape. But it wasn't impossible, and if Jacob could learn to live with himself afterward, he would keep these secrets with him to the end. Should Ruth ever come to suspect him, to speak out would be to risk exposing *herself*; no, she'd never say a word. Of that Jacob was willing to bet everything.

He'd spent the entirety of the next Saturday on the second floor of the public library; they had a secondary computer lab up there, one that was always less crowded than the one on ground level. Andy was having a girl's day with some of her lingering friends from college, so he wouldn't be interrupted. He'd dressed himself as unremarkably as possible in a generic sweatshirt and jeans, the plainest shoes he owned, and a black beanie that covered all of his hair, despite the persistent warmth of the weather. He even left his phone at home, just in case; if ever there was a time for caution, it was now.

There had been a corner of the lab that wasn't in the line of vision for any of the room's security cameras, and Jacob took advantage, choosing a computer that would keep his face out of the security feed. Opening the internet browser in Incognito mode, he'd gorged himself on research, reaffirming and adding to his knowledge on Reshawl hollies, the toxin, what it could be combined with, and known symptoms and side-effects. Instead of printing out pages, he copied and pasted it all into one text document, saving it on a flash drive he'd bought, with cash, for the occasion.

If anyone else had known what he was doing, they would have called him paranoid. Wasn't his *mother* the paranoid one? Or, perhaps, like mother like son.

He'd brushed that thought aside.

An hour before Andy was due to return home, as he pushed back from the computer and rubbed his aching eyes, Jacob had felt confident he'd gathered every bit of information there was to find in public record regarding Reshawl holly trees.

The Harmeling office was on his way home. They were closed on weekends, so the chances of bumping into someone were slim to none. There had been a delay in shipping the Reshawl holly, something to do with the buyer, but Jacob hadn't been afforded a clean opportunity to get close to it during work hours. The tree was scheduled to finally leave the warehouse on Monday morning; this would likely be his last shot.

He took it.

Jacob bypassed the security system to get inside the office, taking care to use the code of one of his managers rather than his own, and made his way to the back warehouse where the tree was being stored. He collected what he needed from near the base, an area that had already suffered some peeling during the removal process. He worked fast, sealing the bark in a large plastic bag when he deemed what he'd gathered as enough for experimentation and reproduction. Another five minutes and he was back in the car without episode, headed home to welcome Andy back.

The bag of Reshawl holly bark lay full on the passenger seat beside him as if in waiting.

The weeks after were spent in an agonizing cycle of trial and error as he perfected the toxin. Doing it out of the way of Andy presented a completely separate challenge, but in the early mornings before Andy woke up for work, bent over a card table in a storage unit he rented with cash, Jacob made it work.

He needed a way to administer the toxin indirectly to John, something infallible. He landed eventually on letters. It was something tangible John could fixate on, and that was an important aspect to the plan. Perhaps he would think it strange to suddenly receive letters in the mail from his

Generation-X grandson, especially considering their distant relationship, but the man was bound to be lonely after the death of his wife. He would be in that huge house all alone now. There would be little to keep him from accepting companionship in this uncommitted, introverted way, Jacob was convinced.

The only concern was what would happen to the letters after they were opened—no one else could find them, or the whole scheme could come undone. It was this problem that helped Jacob to choose his final mixture for the toxin. Efer-alchloralide would cause severe side-effects of paranoia, difficulty distinguishing time, obsession and or fixation, and hoarding—struggles not uncommon among seniles. It was the ideal cover.

The mixture would be in powder form, dusted onto the pages of Jacob's letters to John. The envelopes would be safe for any handlers. The risks were few: John throwing the letters away after reading them, in which case, he would be destroying the murder weapons on Jacob's behalf; however, if the hoarding side-effect manifested strongly in John, Jacob could have a trying time locating the letters after John's death.

After consideration, Jacob determined the possibility a necessary risk.

He kept the letters as pleasant but basic as possible; after all, he was murdering the old man as he read—no amount of kind things said would make up for it. He sent them bi-weekly for ten months before the news came through the family grapevine that John had passed in his sleep. It was the way most people wished to go; he was fortunate not to have suffered.

Before the funeral, Jacob received the first call from Michael Marsden. He'd anticipated hearing from John's lawyer with word on the will, but the last thing he'd expected was to get the house *and* the money.

"John called me a few weeks before he died," Mr. Marsden had told him, "like he knew he was going soon. He insisted I change the will to benefit you more, and gave me highly specific instructions on how to do it."

It was an irony not lost on Jacob that the very letters he'd used to poison John had also been the thing that put him higher in his grandfather's esteem.

The house even came with its own nest egg for remodeling. John and Betty had lived such simple lives, Marsden declared, and they saved every spare coin, never giving thought to elaborate luxuries. It left them with a lot to pass down.

So his grandparents had not been exaggerating to him about the nest egg, and yet he'd managed to secure even more than that in the end.

He'd had to pinch himself to make sure it was all really happening.

Jacob didn't share with Andy the details of the call in any capacity except for the precise amount of the prior allotment they'd known they would get. Even then, she was floored. "I can't believe they were sitting on so much money all these years! I envy that level of discipline."

Not long after, Andy was offered an interview at a new office, a better office, with higher pay and improved benefits. Her stress levels skyrocketed, making her a little crazy. Her panic attacks tripled. After the second interview, she started talking about a new apartment; their lease on the current one was almost up. If she got this new job, wouldn't an apartment across town be so much better than where they were now, an hour from Harmeling in rush hour traffic, an hour from both offices for her?

The longer Jacob waited to mention the house, the position it put him in became less and less desirable. When Andy got the new job, she pestered him into apartment shopping and claimed to fall in love with the first one they looked at. Jacob convinced her to wait on signing any papers, to make sure she really loved the new job first.

Later that same week, she went on her lunch hour to the complex and started signing papers for a lease. It was a surprise, she told Jacob that evening. She thought he loved the apartment as much as she did, that he was just dragging his feet in case she changed her mind. He promised her he would drive over and finish signing for the lease the following week. Instead, he had to explain the situation to the complex manager over the phone. She wasn't too pleased, but she shredded the half-signed lease.

Jacob fought to steer clear of Ruth until she finally cornered him at John's wake. She blasted him for taking on the house, not letting the siblings sell it off and split the profits. He reminded her about the stipulations of the will, that whoever took the house couldn't sell it, or their claim to it would not only be voided, but they'd lose their entire inheritance. She changed her strategy then, made out like she had his best interests at heart, that it would be better if she took the house off his hands so there would be no burden for he and Andy; but when he told her about Andy's new job and how her office would be within seven miles of the house, Ruth had a conniption, calling him a limp-noodled ninny for letting someone else tell him what to do and where to live—another irony, and one he took pleasure in pointing out to her. As long as she got her money, he knew she would slink back into her hole eventually.

Thus far, Jacob had successfully avoided his guilt. Even seeing his grandfather's waxen face in the casket hadn't made him rethink his decision. It had been a necessary evil, a desperate move for a desperate man—he continued to justify it that way. He'd take a long look at Andy's face while she slept, and he'd say to himself, "This is why...."

That was before he saw the inside of the house. The moment they'd opened up that door, he'd felt the first tendril of regret prick his heart like a pin. Going through his grandparents' things that day, sorting their life into piles, seeing the kitchen scattered with rat droppings, the piles of rubbish halfway up the walls in every room, the very weapons that killed John tied together with string like a treasure, hidden in a safe place within arm's reach of John's final resting place... it was almost too much.

For the first time since he'd killed his grandfather, standing there in the center of John's house, Jacob cried for him. He cried for Patsy, too, who up until today, had been dead from natural causes.

But Jacob knew better now; Andy had no idea what she'd revealed when she told him of Patsy's aneurysm, but the information had slammed into him with all the force of a battering ram.

Hephyraptorol and the toxin were likely to cause an aneurysm; it was on the list of side-effects Jacob knew by heart. He didn't know why she'd done it, but he knew it with the same confidence that he knew the colors of the sky and the sun and the grass: Ruth was responsible for Patsy's death, too. She couldn't have done it for money, because Patsy didn't have any. The only thing that made sense was his mother's insanity, her narcissism. That Patsy was receiving too much attention; Ruth had been pregnant at the time, after all, and shouldn't pregnant mothers-to-be get all the attention?

Could it have been a motive as simple as that?

According to Dirk, she'd always been jealous of Patsy. Maybe that had been reason enough in Ruth's crazed rational.

But the evidence lined up. Ruth would have had access to the same Reshawl holly back in the 80s, because she'd lived next door for years. Whether she had made the toxin years before and stashed it away for a rainy day, or whether she paid a visit to the Blasdells during her pregnancy and snuck over to the neighboring yard to steal the bark, it didn't matter. The result was the same.

Now, Jacob rested his head against the door to the lounge as more tears came for the aunt he would never know. He had no right to cry, not for her, not for John, Betty, or anyone. He was no better than Ruth, and he knew that. One day he'd answer for his crimes. Maybe not in this life, he thought, but he would pay the price.

Suddenly filled with compassion for those pushed prematurely into their deathbeds, Jacob straightened himself. With a roll of his shoulders, a few swipes across his bleary eyes, and a stern set to his jaw, he reached into his pocket and yanked out the keyring. The yellow-spotted key wasn't hard to find. He shoved it into the lock in the door and turned, letting the door swing open on its own. The light from the hallway cast a stark stream across the wooden floor, falling partially across the sheeted figure lying on the table in the center of the room. The repellent smell enveloped him once again, sending bile up the back of his throat, but this time he didn't allow himself to think about it for more than a hasty second.

He stepped forward on steady legs, but his gloved hands were balled into fists as he came astride the table. The white sheet was the only thing between him and the decaying body. With deliberation, he reached out, hand slowly descending to the edge of the sheet. Sucking in his lips with a deep breath, Jacob lifted it towards him, pulling it down and away.

A fresh tear leaked from Jacob's eye as he looked into the shriveled, sunken sockets where Betty's eyes had been in life.

"I'm sorry, Gamma. I never meant for this to happen, but it's all my fault."

The vision of his grandmother from the courthouse when he was eight…that was how he wanted to remember her always.

Jacob peered around the dark lounge, and on a whim, grabbed a book from the shelf—one with a smooth pink cover and a French title in lilting cursive—then one of the tea cups, one he now saw was painted with the friendliest flowers he'd ever seen. With careful movements, he wrapped what was left of Betty into the sheets, setting the book and cup on top of the bundle.

When he was old and weathered in soul and in sanity, if Andy should go to her grave before him, Jacob could not promise himself that he wouldn't want her close to him, as John had wanted Betty. Despite the grotesqueness of digging up the buried corpse of your spouse and then laying it to rest on a table inside your home, there was something poetic and romantic in the act.

Jacob knew what he must do for Betty now. He would return her to her plot at the cemetery—tonight, on foot. In the darkness, no one would see him. It wasn't far, a straight shot from the backyard. He would lay her to rest beside her John, her Lone Ranger. Granddaddy would have wanted that, if he'd been in his right mind.

If he'd been in his right mind, Jacob, he wouldn't have dug her up in the first place. No thanks to you….

"I will live with my demons. That is my punishment until I meet my own grave." The words were staccato as they bounced off the walls of the lounge, crystallizing against Jacob's body like a glass straight-jacket.

As he trod the length of the hallway to open the back door before carrying the body out, arms swinging passively at his sides, he paused in the cross-laden foyer.

All those crosses...they made him think of judgment, reckoning, of lightning streaking toward the land from the heavens. He thought of the world breaking open, of the earth split in two. Then he noticed something he hadn't before: next to his coat still hanging on the sconce, there were crosses with names.

He moved closer, reading:

John Cross

Betty Cross

Patsy Cross

Larry Cross

Ruth Cross

Dirk Cross

Jacob Cross Tamblyn

Brushing his fingers across his own name, Jacob closed his eyes.

One day I'll pay the price for what I've done.

Head bowed, Jacob Cross Tamblyn shuffled to the back door, and opened it to the frigid night air.

AUTHOR'S NOTE

In 2016, unprecedented rainfall resulted in a flood of catastrophic proportions in the southern parts of Louisiana. Many families, including my own, experienced the devastation firsthand. During the aftermath and clean-up efforts, one of the biggest eye-openers for me was a rather unexpected one: the realization of just how much "stuff" we accumulate — meaningless stuff that serves little or no purpose besides taking up space. It took over a year to manifest, but the initial concept of *Wall of Crosses* was born from this revelation.

Since I am a discovery writer, the story branched out with slow, unfurling roots, eventually becoming far more deep and convoluted than I'd planned. When I first brainstormed and outlined, I had one simple goal: throw together a short story. Just do it.

Well, I thought to myself, if a short story I must write, then it should be a really powerful one! So my attitude shifted to challenging myself: I would write a short story that was unlike anything I'd written before. Instead of feel-good warm fuzzies at the end, instead of more likable characters than not, instead of redemption, instead of neat bows to tie everything up at the end...I wanted to do the opposite.

So I asked myself what gets people talking. Is it stuff that ends nicely, predictably? No! It's the NOT-happy endings that seem to leave the most poignant impressions, right? The prospect of going that direction totally excited me. I longed to write that story — the one that wasn't a cookie cutter of something we've seen a million times, something that broke the mold a little.

Spring-boarding off my personal post-flood experiences and those of people close to me, I moved on to inspiration for character dynamics. Next came figuring out a setting that would force those characters together, and then I had to figure out how to shake things up for them. Then the big question came to me: "What would it look like to have a story in which everything does wrap up neatly at the end, but for the killer?" It's not often we see a story in which all the wrong people get what they want in the end. Where the criminal walks away scot free — in this case, when no one even suspects he is a criminal!

I guess it's fitting that this book took on the tone it did; I am naturally drawn to tales with meaty themes, so it makes sense I'd write one that falls into that category. It's my hope that the bleak ending of this story resonates with people, makes them think. Some readers may see *Wall of Crosses* as a story of despair, but it was intended as a picture of total depravity without Christ, of what it is to give into sin, and to live in darkness. Jacob essentially gets away with "the perfect crime", and we not only don't catch it (as the reader), but we root for him! While there's something a little delicious in that kind of sly deception (since readers aren't often hood-winked that way), in reality, this wouldn't be a pleasant dupe at all. Yet it's exactly how Satan operates.

From a certain viewpoint, it could be argued that Jacob

himself is a bit Satan-esque: a decent guy on the surface, harmless enough, and it's easy to get sucked into his seemingly straightforward persona — but in the end, everything about him is a lie. He was the ultimate deceiver of the story.

I purposely ended the narrative where I did because I wanted readers to imagine what would happen next on their own. How will the rest of Jacob's days pan out? Do you think he will come to regret his choices? Will he be crushed under the weight of his guilt? Will he turn inward on himself and embrace more darkness?

Sometimes sin looks too good to pass up, or like it's the only way. But it's empty, and it brings death — even if it's shaped like a life raft. Thankfully there is one true hope here, one truth: the cross.

For God so loved the world, that He gave His only Son, that whoever believes in Him should not perish but have eternal life. For God did not send His Son into the world to condemn the world, but in order that the world might be saved through Him. Whoever believes in Him is not condemned, but whoever does not believe is condemned already, because he has not believed in the name of the only Son of God. And this is the judgment: the light has come into the world, and people loved the darkness rather than the light because their works were evil. For everyone who does wicked things hates the light and does not come to the light, lest his works should be exposed. But whoever does what is true comes to the light, so that it may be clearly seen that his works have been carried out in God.

— JOHN 3:16-21 ESV

ACKNOWLEDGMENTS

There are *so many* wonderful souls who have touched my life, who've helped me in various ways throughout this crazy journey toward fulfilling my lifelong dream of publishing a book. I have to get long-winded with this, because I can't just NOT thank you guys...

To my WhimsiGals writing group, Adelaide Thorne, Daphne Tatum, and Rebecca McCoy: The impact you all have made on me is truly astounding. I'm monumentally blessed to know you ladies. Not only have you treated WoC like your own book baby, pushing and plugging for it like nobody's business, but you've breathed new life into me as a writer. I've learned so much from each of you — it's, like, a daily thing! How you guys are so magic with the words is just whoa! But even better than that, you guys went from sweet strangers on Instagram to becoming some of my dearest friends. I LOVE YOUR SMILING FACES! I'll always treasure our bond, and I can't wait to see where the future takes us! Thank you for every. single. word. out of your charming mouths. Thank you for investing in me, not only as a writer and #bookstagrammer, but as a friend and as a person. You gals are my favorite constellation.

To Ashley Baker of Ashes Books & Bobs Blog: Omg, girl, where do I start with you?! You were my first advocate once I started rebranding myself as an author, and you've never let up! Your friendship is one of my most cherished, and I'm so glad I get to galavant around in the book world with you. Thank you for always believing in me, even when I didn't, and thank you for never letting me quit on myself. Your words of encouragement and support have gotten me through many a low-point, so in a big way, you're one of the reasons this book exists! How 'bout dem apples?! And thank you for reading this book as a 3-star first draft, because it spurred me on to make it better. You're a rockstar teammate, girl. Thank you for being there.

To Tyffany Hackett: Thank you for being so open to discussing all the ins and outs of the hot-mess self-publishing world with me. I would have drowned without your advice! And furthermore, thank you for being an inspiration. It was because of you that I knew I could do this without a publisher. You showed me it could really be done. *Hugs*

To my beta and ARC readers: You guys are what authorly dreams are made of. Thank you for loving on my book and sharing it with the world.

To my booksta friends: I wouldn't be here without you guys. Seriously. All of you, as a collective, gave me wings. Like, I'm not even sorry for putting that phrase in writing.

To Tim Gabrielle: Thanks for being my first author buddy, for the periodic check-ins and authentic writing encouragement, and for inspiring me to write a heck of a lot faster than I naturally do because of your crazy-fast pace, dude!

To my Oaks Church family: Thank you for your invaluable prayers and encouragement, and for keeping my spiritual feet on the ground. Thank you for the community, the growth, and for doing life with me.

To Dean and Ricky Stewart: Y'all are pretty much my unsung heroes (and benefactors). Thanks for all you do for my family (including putting up with my husband five days a week!).

To Josh Belgard: Thank you for ALLTHETHINGS!!! You are our mercy solider!

To Mrs. Melinda Partin: You deserve special mention, lady. Your eyes didn't glaze over ONCE when I talked about the writing process! Thank you for all the times you asked about my progress out of genuine interest, not just for the sake of small talk. You make me feel ten feet tall.

To Josh Guilbeau: You're a machine, man. Thank you for not only making my cover dreams a reality, but for doing it in record time! You da real MVP.

To Chelsea Faith, A-1: Thank you for keeping me supplied with memes, inappropriate Tweets, BuzzFeed articles, Snaps, Bitmoji funnies, and bestie talk. It's almost (almost!) as good as having you with me through the daily grind. I miss you, sister.

To Shelby Moy, Emily Ward, and Amber Bourgeois: Your texts, voice chats, and Marco Polos give me life. Thank y'all for not letting me slide completely under the friend radar when I get buried in to-do lists and self-inflicted deadlines. I wuv you!

To my family-in-love, Donnie, Maureen, Keith, Casey, and Anna: Thank you for not freaking out when I quit my job to write books like an insane person. Y'all are the epitome of supportive. I'm so thankful for each and every one of you!

To Tommy, Elliott, and Aveline: Thank you for making my heart warm on Sunday afternoons so I could recharge my feelings-meter for a new week of character-driven writing! All my love.

To my family tree, the Jordans, Blues, Elliotts, Akins, Davises, Steinkes, etc.: Thank y'all for not being murderous psychopaths for one, but also for believing in me every step of the way — always. Throughout my entire life. None of you ever told me I was being childish or too idealistic when I dreamed big. You never tried to stifle me, to slyly suggest I shouldn't pursue my goals, even as they changed over the years. You've all been telling me "you absolutely can" since the day I was born. I thank God the Cross family is purely a figment of my imagination, that none of their craziness came from any of you — because my family is pretty stinkin' great!

To Eden Dove and Gideon Kennedy: Thank you for making me laugh, and for giving me such great photo material to use as backgrounds on my Insta Stories. BamBam loves you both!

Now to my limbs...

To Daddy, Momma, and Julz: The Merry, Pippin, and Samwise to my Frodo. I don't know who I am without you, because every bit of me is wrapped up in you. You are my kindred spirits, my oldest friends, and my most sacred of treasures. No amount of pretty prose would do any of you justice, but still — thank you for never giving up on me, for lifting me up so high that I finally know the magic of holding the moon in my hands. It's because of you, all of you, that I am anything at all. I love you endlessly.

To Mark: I save you for last (well, second to last) because that place is reserved for the foundation of my castle. I will never be able to thank you enough for all that you are, and all that you've done. Thank you for not taking off and never coming back like one Harrison Tamblyn, because I know I've been a monster during this whole book process! (I really don't do stress very well, do I?) You've loved me through my worst moments over the past eleven months, and that was no easy feat. What's more, you were the instigator of this life-changing author journey, the one who told me "go", the one who supported me readily when I launched us into the unknown. You took on so many heavy burdens, like a friggin' legit martyr, and you did it so I could pursue my wildest dreams. That takes a special kind of person, babe. I definitely owe you some Swiss Cake Rolls (and probably a few kisses, too). You are a saint, my love, and you will always have my heart.

And last but not least...

To you, dear reader: Thank you for allowing me to entangle you in my storytelling web. There is no greater pleasure for a writer, of that I'm convinced. I hope you enjoyed reading this tale as much as I enjoyed creating it. May our minds meld again someday!

With love,
Baj

~

ABOUT THE AUTHOR

Baj (like 'badge', but without the -*d*) Goodson is a Texas native transplanted in Louisiana with her hubby and two feral Chorkies. She's a twenty-something old soul, an avid reader, pipe-dream baker, Netflix couch potato, and a former school teacher with a Bachelor of the Arts degree in English Language Arts from the University of Texas at Tyler. After spending her life fantasizing being a fiction writer, it wasn't until 2017 that she took the plunge, quit her job as a robot, and pursued writing as a career (with greater risk comes greater reward?). She loves it, by the way. *Wall of Crosses* is her first published work.

Follower of Jesus Christ. Wife. Dog mom. Connoisseur of desserts. Lover of artsy things. Infinite dreamer.

Sign up for Baj's newsletter for first-looks at future publications, freebies, exclusive story extras, TBR recommendations, life updates, & more.
https://bit.ly/2M1TKo4

Connect with Baj:
Email | baj@goodsoninnovations.com
Website | bajgoodson.com
Wattpad | wattpad.com/user/bajgoodson

facebook.com/bajgoodsonauthor

twitter.com/bajgoodson

instagram.com/bajgoodson

goodreads.com/bajgoodson

pinterest.com/bajgoodson

ALSO BY BAJ GOODSON

Want more from this author?

Check out the FREE Young Adult serial on WATTPAD.com
Read now!

Seventeen-year-old Kris Harmon thinks the worst that could happen to her would be A) scaring off her long-time crush Aaron Arsane, who is finally interested in her after years of pining, or B) being stifled by her overprotective father when things with Aaron are just getting started. But when one fateful fight with her dad leads to a life-changing trauma no one could have foreseen, Kris's life spins out of control — and her only hope is to find something beautiful in the ashes.

A STORY OF GRACE, SACRIFICE, & UNCONDITIONAL LOVE